DRACULA IN ISTANBUL

BRAM STOKER
ALİ RIZA SEYFİOĞLU

TRANSLATED FROM THE TURKISH BY
NECİP ATEŞ

EDITED BY
ED GLASER

FOREWORD BY **KIM NEWMAN**
INTRODUCTION BY **ŞEHNAZ TAHİR GÜRÇAĞLAR**
AFTERWORD BY **IAIN ROBERT SMITH**

This edition first published in the United States in 2017 by Neon Harbor Entertainment, LLC.

ISBN: 0692918418
ISBN-13: 978-0692918418

Published by:
Neon Harbor Entertainment, LLC
neonharbor.com
info@neonharbor.com

CONTENTS

FOREWORD

by Kim Newman

In my collection of editions of *Dracula*, I have versions of
Bram Stoker's 1897 novel rewritten in English for various
readerships… comic books, film scripts, plays. A Pop-Up
Dracula and illustrated retellings for younger readers are at one
end of the shelf… at the other are editions with newly-added
sex scenes ("a piece of ass is a piece of ass—be it in England
or here in Transylvania" begins Jonathan Harker's diary in *The
Adult Version of Dracula*, published by Calga Books in 1970).
Only now, a hundred and twenty years after Stoker's book
came out, are we beginning to explore the non-English
language variants of the founding text of modern horror.

In an afterword to *Powers of Darkness: The Lost Version of
Dracula* (Duckworth Overlook, 2017)—a translation into
English of *Makt Myrkanna*, Valdimar Ásmundsson's free
Icelandic adaptation (1900) of Bram Stoker's *Dracula* (1987)—
John Edgar Browning suggests "unearthing translations like
Makt Myrkanna may become the next cottage industry in
Dracula scholarship and entertainment." The appearance in a
new English translation of *Kazıklı Voyvoda/The Impaling Voivode*
proves his case. That a book as well-known as *Dracula* should
exist in such altered versions from territories as far apart as

Iceland and Turkey indicates something unique about this particular work (and character).

Given that this is an area of literary scholarship which has been neglected, it remains to be seen whether other popular works of this vintage—Oscar Wilde's *The Picture of Dorian Gray* (1891), H.G. Wells's *The War of the Worlds* (1898), Henry James's *The Turn of the Screw* (1898), Joseph Conrad's *Heart of Darkness* (1902), Arthur Conan Doyle's *The Hound of the Baskervilles* (1902), or Gaston Leroux's *The Phantom of the Opera* (1911)—have such extreme variants. Is there an Egyptian *War of the Worlds* where the Martian War Machines stride past pyramids to lay waste to Cairo… a Polish Phantom lurking under a Budapest Opera House… a Japanese sleuth unmasking a cat ghost as the scheming heir to a title and fortune? Certainly, when the movies got hold of these key texts, there would be room for a Chinese *Phantom of the Opera* (*Ye ban ge sheng/A Song at Midnight*, 1937), multiple American-set *Wars of the Worlds* from Orson Welles's radio play through to films by Byron Haskin and Steven Spielberg, a Hindi *Hound of the Baskervilles* (*Bees Saal Baad/Twenty Years Later*, 1962), and a *Heart of Darkness* set during the Vietnam War (*Apocalypse Now*, 1979). But Dracula seems uniquely mutable, as attested to by the emergence of long-known-about, hitherto-hard-to-assess translations/adaptations/reinventions.

Outside Turkey, Ali Rıza Seyfioğlu's *Kazıklı Voyvoda* first became heard of when people writing books about vampire films—Barrie Pattinson (*The Seal of Dracula*, 1975), James Ursini and Alain Silver (*The Vampire Film*, 1975), David Pirie (*The Vampire Cinema*, 1977)—made mention of Mehmet Muhtar's *Drakula İstanbul'da* (1953), a film they knew of but which was then unseen in Europe and America. Donald F. Glut's *The Dracula Book* (1975) includes a synopsis of the film and a still of Atif Kaptan as a Dracula with the bald pate of Max Schreck in *Nosferatu, eine symphonie das grauens* (1922) and cape-and-evening-wear costume of Bela Lugosi in *Dracula* (1931) but also the prominent fangs which wouldn't catch on in Western movies until Christopher Lee bared his teeth in *Dracula* (1958). Glut states that "the film was based both upon Stoker's *Dracula* and upon the novel *Kasîgli Voyvoda*, by Ali Riga Seifi." It wasn't until Pete Tombs's *Mondo Macabro* (1997) that anyone wrote in English about *Drakula İstanbul'da* after actually seeing the film. Then, it was only around as an unsubtitled bootleg VHS recorded off Turkish television. Now, though the print quality hasn't improved, the film is on YouTube with English subtitles—though some blunt translations add a layer of humor probably not intended by the filmmakers. "I read your book on vampires. I think Miss Şadan is a sucker. She must be the one sucking little kids in Eyup." "Turan, I know you loved her deeply, but she is a bogey now." "We should go and garlic the chests before midnight."

Drakula İstanbul'da can now be assessed as an important stage of the evolution of *Dracula* as a film property. For all that it's an adaptation not of Stoker but of *Kazıklı Voyvoda*—using (most of) the character names Seyfioğlu invented and shifting the location from London to Turkey—*Drakula İstanbul'da* follows Bram Stoker's plot more faithfully than the other four film adaptations of the novel made in the first sixty years of the 20th century. Among other things, Muhtar is the first filmmaker to stage Stoker's memorable image of the Count crawling head-first down the wall of his castle. Though, of course, Muhtar wasn't necessarily adapting Stoker's book—his film is based much more closely on Seyfioğlu's. Like Tod Browning in 1931, Muhtar (working from a script by Ümit Deniz) opts for a contemporary setting rather than make a period piece. Stoker's book makes a point of being set roughly in its present day and featuring up to the minute tech like dictographs and blood transfusions, and wouldn't accrue the patina of Victoriana until Hammer Films started making films set in an era of gaslight and hansom cabs. Seyfioğlu set his version (published in 1928) in the 1920s and made the characters' involvement in the then-recent Turkish War of Independence (1919-23) a crucial part of their backstory. Muhtar opts for an understated 1950s setting, with motorcars and nightclub scenes, even to the commercial extent of making Seyfioğlu's patriotic and pure

Mina character Güzin a dancer who desports in a harem outfit and is hypnotized by Dracula into giving the vampire a saucy private performance before the heroes stake and behead him. The novel excludes all humor—even Stoker's comic relief rustics and occasional jabs at Van Helsing's silly accent and Renfield's grotesque habits—but the film ends with the vampire-hunting hero secure enough in the monster's death to insist his new wife throw all the garlic out of the house and never use it in cooking again.

In 1900, Ásmundsson created his *Dracula* for a newspaper serial, which forced him to deliver short episodes with cliffhangers—but he was inclined for some reason to add his own sub-plots and characters, combining Dracula's three wives into one temptress who might be the historical Countess Elisabeth Bathory and predating Hammer's later films by giving his Dracula a cult of acolytes, minions, well-connected disciples and a penchant for murderous sacrificial rituals. He also seems to have decided after a year which barely got him past the Transylvania section of the novel to wrap things up quickly. Seyfioğlu can't possibly have known about *Makt Myrkanna* when he set out to turn *Dracula* into something else, though he may have been aware of F.W. Murnau's film *Nosferatu*—which changed the character names and set the story in Bremen in a bid to evade copyright—and even of London and Broadway stage adaptations by Hamilton Deane and John F. Balderston, which took their own liberties with the novel and established a framework that Browning would work on when he was put in charge of Universal's *Dracula*. It cannot have escaped him that Count Dracula had long since escaped from Stoker, who died in 1912, and become—despite the widow Florence Stoker's waving of writs and claiming of royalties—what we might now call an "open-source" text.

In Turkey, as in Romania, the name *Dracula* meant something before 1897 and Stoker's novel had to compete with the lasting reputation of Vlad the Impaler, also known as Dracula. It wasn't until Radu Florescu and Raymond T. McNally's *In Search of Dracula* (1972) that anything much was made of the relationship between the literary and historical Draculas in the Western world—though the lasting influence of this by-no-means-uncontentious book is felt on almost all subsequent literary and film Draculas. In Turkey, the Florescu-McNally contention that Dracula *was* Vlad the Impaler was old news, cemented by Seyfioğlu's book. It strikes me, after quite a bit of research, that Stoker mostly just liked the name Dracula and probably knew little about Vlad beyond the skimpy, not-entirely-accurate historical details he mentions (to be fair, his Dracula is an unreliable narrator). Seyfioğlu, writing for a readership with more awareness of Turkish-Romanian history, makes much more of the Vlad connection and, indeed, includes historical details and anecdotes which feature in *In Search of Dracula* and have been recycled over and over in fiction, documentary, history, and film ever since. How many times have you heard the turbans-nailed-to-heads story or seen the forest-of-impaled-enemies tableau?

For Bram Stoker, Dracula is an ultimate foreign threat (likened to Attila, a barbarian not only from the geographic East but the historic past) who comes to London with his ill-gotten riches (when stabbed, he bleeds gold coins), apes British manners (memorising railway timetables) and dress ("a straw hat which suit him not") and sets out to seduce the fairest daughters of Albion (Lucy and Mina). That Stoker, an Irishman, includes an American cowboy and a Dutch Professor in his array of mostly English heroes suggests his own notions of Western civilisation are broader than the average Brit of his day, though Quincy Morris and Dr. Van Helsing are, for all their qualities as stalwart and wise, "funny foreigner" stereotypes too. Seyfioğlu is even more bluntly propagandist. Dracula is an old enemy, and a disgusting threat, and the good guys are all emblematic Turks, free of the flaws (like Dr. Seward's drug abuse) Stoker allows his heroes. Quincy becomes Özdemir Oğuz, an Anatolian whose swashbuckling outdoorsy persona makes him roughly analogous to a Wild West gunslinger/cowman… while Van Helsing is Resuhî Bey, a Turkish expert in mental illnesses acknowledged even in

France as a credit to his nation. Seyfioğlu also has to Islamicize the action, though the Transylvania sections of the book feature Christian crosses as per Stoker—this vampire is seen off by verses from the Koran rather than communion wafers.

Upon its first appearance, few realized how significant a book *Dracula* would be. It was respectfully reviewed, sold reasonably well without making its author rich, and lingered in the memory long enough to attract theatre and film adaptors a generation later. Only Bram Stoker's mother—who might have been prejudiced—suggested that it was an instant horror classic ("Poe is nowhere," she wrote to Bram). In his lifetime, he was responsible for a cut-and-paste first theater version (supposedly to secure copyright), saw the book translated and reprinted, and might have begun to sense that it would last— though he made few attempts to capitalize on it, despite writing another vampire novel (sort of—*The Lady of the Shroud*). "Dracula's Guest," an offcut from the book, didn't appear until after his death, when Florence began to sense that *Dracula* might afford her a widow's pension. But Dracula remains undead—an evolving, mutating, constantly self-referential multi-media text, yet also a cornerstone contemporary myth. *Dracula*'s career in English has been thoroughly mapped, but— as John Edgar Browning noted, vast areas beyond that are still unexplored. With this translation of a translation, a significant patch of the collage is filled in. Many more remain.

INTRODUCTION

by Şehnaz Tahir Gürçağlar

Bram Stoker's *Dracula* is a text that has had many resurrections and reincarnations around the world, in many languages, through various print and visual media. The novel has endured the eroding effects of time and continues to appeal to radically different readerships than it was initially intended for. Now, in the 21st century, it is stronger than ever, and Count Dracula is a figure recognized by all—even those who have not read the novel or seen the screen versions. It is funny how the book seems to have come closer to what Count Dracula has lost forever: an immortal life—at least for over a century. To me, *Dracula*'s resilience owes to the way it has let itself be ingested and cannibalized in various translations, adaptations, and rewrites—only to emerge stronger from each ordeal. The Turkish adaptation you are about to read in English translation is only one aspect of the larger *Dracula* picture, but it is one that perfectly illustrates the transformative power of translation in multiplying the lives of a literary work in different cultures.

Ali Rıza Seyfioğlu's *Kazıklı Voyvoda*, the source text of *Dracula in Istanbul: The Unauthorized Version of the Gothic Classic*, was published in Istanbul for the first time in Ottoman script in 1928, shortly before the alphabet reform that led to the adoption of Latin letters and irrevocably transformed the cultural landscape in the newly-founded Republic of Turkey. Although a close comparison reveals that the book is indeed a translation of *Dracula*, it was presented as an original Turkish novel, and Ali Rıza Seyfi (as he was sometimes known) was indicated on the cover as the author. In 1946, the novel was reprinted in the Latin alphabet. The second edition preserved the content and structure of the first edition, while the Ottoman vocabulary was modified to reflect the changes the Turkish language had undergone in the eighteen years that had elapsed. There is no clear information as to why Ali Rıza Seyfi claimed to be the author of the book and why he did not introduce it as a translation. I assume that he considered the text as a fruitful ground upon which he could build a historical novel drawing on Ottoman sources and readily appropriated the structure, plot, and characters of *Dracula* to further his own literary and ideological aspirations. Moreover, the changes he made to the text were too comprehensive to present it as a conventional translation.

Kazıklı Voyvoda was not only produced and received as an indigenous novel; it was also adapted to the screen. Ümit Deniz, a popular writer of detective fiction, wrote a script based on *Kazıklı Voyvoda*, and the film *Dracula İstanbul'da* (Dracula in Istanbul) was released in 1953. The credit titles of the film explicitly acknowledged Ali Rıza Seyfi as the author of the book. You can read more about the film in the afterword to this book. *Kazıklı Voyvoda* was reprinted in 1997 under the title *Dracula İstanbul'da*, this time accompanied by a preface by late Giovanni Scognamillo, who formally identified the translation status of the novel for the first time. Nevertheless, the readers were clearly already aware of this, as the title of the film alluded to *Dracula* rather than *Kazıklı Voyvoda*.

In his translation, Ali Rıza Seyfi renamed the novel *Kazıklı Voyvoda* and associated it right from the start with an evil figure from Ottoman history.[1] This is a feature that created some

---

1   Turkish for "Vlad the Impaler." Vlad Dracula, who reigned briefly as the voivode of Wallachia in the 15th century, was known for his cruel

authenticity and built a historical context for the novel. This context enabled the author to use his translation as a platform through which he relayed his version of Ottoman-Turkish history and addressed a strong nationalist sentiment.

In *Kazıklı Voyvoda*, Ali Rıza Seyfi retained the narrative structure of *Dracula* by keeping the epistolary style and using diary entries as the main narrative tool. The plot is also quite similar to that of *Dracula*, with the exception of a number of omissions and additions.[2] Ali Rıza Seyfi domesticated the setting and moved the story to Istanbul, while he also gave the characters Turkish names and equipped them with a number of new traits associated with heroism and patriotism. The additions Ali Rıza Seyfi made to the novel mainly served to evoke nationalist feelings in the readership. These additions create a sense of shared history and continuity between the heroic deeds of the former Ottoman army and the Turkish population of the 1920s. The fight against Count Dracula in Stoker's original novel has often been read as a fight between the good and evil forces of human nature. Ali Rıza Seyfi turns this fight into a national one and has his characters finish off the battles raged against Vlad the Impaler by Ottoman forces centuries ago. In return, these historical references stand as a metaphor for a more recent national struggle—that of the Turkish War of Independence, which had only been over for five years when the novel was first published in Turkey. This subtext can only be understood, and Ali Rıza Seyfi's adaptation properly appreciated, in the light of these historical facts.

Ali Rıza Seyfi's *Kazıklı Voyvoda* is more than a historical curiosity—it demonstrates the manipulative power of a translator and a translation in its most acute form. Yet, it also recreates Dracula in a new historical and cultural context and by doing so, joins the giant vortex of Dracula representations that breathe new life into the work. We know that Ali Rıza Seyfi was not unique in his attempts at radically rewriting Dracula for a local readership. Among over thirty translations

---

method of torture whereby he had his victims impaled slowly on stakes.

2   A full Turkish translation of Stoker's *Dracula* did not appear until 1998.

of *Dracula* (see http://www.cesnur.org/2003/dracula/ for an incomplete list), *Kazıklı Voyvoda* was not the only version that reigned free and broke the chains of servitude. A recent book[3] tells the story of the first translation of *Dracula* into any language, the Icelandic *Makt Myrkanna* (Power of Darkness) by Valdimar Ásmundsson. This translation also features extensive omissions, changes and new elements, as well as new characters inserted into the story. Although there are attempts to explain the changes in this particular translation by the fact that Stoker collaborated with Ásmundsson, the degree of involvement by Stoker is unclear, and the line between the authorial interventions of Stoker and Ásmundsson is blurred. It would not be a surprise to discover similar cases in different languages, since *Dracula* seems to tease creative imagination and invites its translation through its polyphonic structure and universal motifs.

The translation you are about to read is a genuine endeavor to reflect *Kazıklı Voyvoda* in its authentic context. Through the use of explanatory footnotes, and the decision to retain some culturally-loaded words untranslated, the translator and editor invite the readers into the world of Turkish culture and history, and make their reading experience all the more enriching. As the translation of a translation, *Dracula in Istanbul: The Unauthorized Version of the Gothic Classic* is a playful text, destabilizing the conventional concepts of "original" and "translation." Which is the original text of the present translation? Is it *Kazıklı Voyvoda*, or should the origins be searched in *Dracula*? This is a wonderful and unsettling example of intertextuality that reverses the direction of textual lineages.

Ali Rıza Seyfi's *Dracula* adaptation is becoming available to an English language readership for the first time thanks to Ed Glaser's personal and painstaking efforts. I hope that it will be the point of departure for many a *Dracula* adventure in the future.

---

3   *Powers of Darkness: The Lost Version of Dracula*, tr. Hans De Roos, Overlook Books, 2017

A NOTE ON THE TRANSLATION

Kazıklı Voyvoda mysteriously stops separating its story into chapters at 6, only about halfway through the book. For easier reading, chapter breaks 7 through 14 have been added. Their placement is suggested by chapter breaks in the original Stoker text.

In Turkish, the suffixes "Bey" and "Hanım" are conventional modes of address for men and women, respectively. They serve much the same purpose as "Mr." and "Ms.," but are used after a person's given name—for example "Azmi Bey" and "Güzin Hanım." Surnames are not normally used in conversation. Hereditary, fixed surnames were also not officially implemented in Turkey until 1934, six years after the first publication of *Kazıklı Voyvoda*.

A Selected Pronunciation Guide

A, a   *o* as in hot

Â, â   faint "y" sound following preceding consonant, or lengthening of "a" sound

C, c   *j* as in jump

Ç, ç   *ch* as in change

G, g   *g* as in get

Ğ, ğ   has no sound, but lengthens preceding vowel slightly

I, ı   *u* as in jump

İ, i   *ee* as in keep

Î, î   extended "i"

O, o   *o* as in off

Ö, ö   *u* as in urge

Ş, ş   *sh* as in shape

U, u   *u* as in put

Ü, ü   *u* as in nude

-ey   *a* as in make

PREFACE

This gruesome and terribly strange adventure, which I have decided to disclose to the world, fell into my hands in the form of a great pile of papers as though it had rained down from the sky. As such, I have not contributed to its writing or editing.

It was an autumn night. I had boarded one of the last ferries from Göztepe to Haydarpaşa. It was very crowded. When we arrived at Haydarpaşa Pier, everyone gathered at the side of the ferry to disembark. I was a little slow because I had been absorbed in my paper. When I stood up from the bench there was no one else around me, but I spied a pile of documents wrapped in old newspaper and picked it up. I wanted to move quickly to deliver it to its owner, but everyone began to rush to the bridge and it was every man for himself. The few people I asked said that the papers did not belong to them. So in the end, the bundle came home with me. The next day I put a public notice in the newspaper with my address. Fifteen days passed, but no one answered. Finally I opened the parcel, which consisted of papers written in several different hands, and read through them. I found myself in a growing state of curiosity and excitement. I would have said that it was a novel, but the pages had been plucked from journals of various shapes and sizes and appeared to have been written by both men and women. All of this added an eerie sense of reality to the adventure.

It appears that the pieces of this adventure had been taken from the diaries of the people involved, and then put into chronological order along with some letters. Did these terrible events, which are the frightening continuation and conclusion of those begun centuries ago, really occur in those desolate, mysterious corners of Istanbul? If not, then what is the meaning of the documents I hold? Those who doubt what I have said may come and see these papers for themselves.

CHAPTER I

FROM THE DIARY OF AZMİ BEY, A YOUNG ISTANBUL
ATTORNEY

3 May. (Town of Bistriç - Transylvania.)—I arrived in Vienna on the second of May. I only briefly glimpsed Budapest from the station, but my impression was that it is built like a gateway from east to west and west to east. Crossing the Danube River, babbling like a living testament to the glorious past of the Turkish nation, my great and famous race, the train carried me to places closely connected with Turkish history. Deep inside me the bitter, sweet, but above all proud and noble feelings fluttered and thrilled me. I felt a great sense of national pride. What a miracle of the soul these feelings are! The sweet, endless immortality of human societies!

Before leaving Istanbul I read with great interest about Transylvania, historically called "Erdel" in Turkish, which saw many bloody war campaigns in our own history and during the recent conflicts in Europe. Not only did it make this unexpected trip more productive and enjoyable, but it may also ease the business of meeting with a Transylvanian noble.

I gathered from my reading that the district this nobleman specified is in the eerie region of the Carpathian Mountains, standing at the easternmost end of Transylvania, on the borders of Moldavia and Bukovina. As I understand from books and maps, this is one of the least known areas of the European continent.

I was not able to find a map indicating Castle Dracula, but the town of Bistriç, which was described by Count Dracula as the postal and communication hub of the region, is indeed a well-known and lively place.

The landscapes I have encountered in this unfamiliar country are such a pleasant addition to my trip. Everywhere I look, I am reminded of Güzin; but it is not as though I ever forgot her in the first place! Ah, dear Güzin… If you were here with me in this wild, ancient land of mountains, amid these odd-looking people with their strange habits; if we could travel, talking together on these lonely roads, how happy and joyous we would be! This is just the life you wanted. In this foreign country, I would feel that you completely belonged to me.

Her curiosity and passionate love of history—especially Turkish history, brimming with epic stories and heroism— would have made this trip invaluable to her. Also, was it not my dear Güzin who, in Istanbul, first drew my attention to the familiar name of Dracula?

Güzin knows better than I do the bloody, horrible, blood-curdling acts that Voivode Dracula committed during the reign of Mehmed II in the history of the Turkish Empire. She has spoken, eyes glistening with tears of rage and excitement, of the tortures of this violent, cruel tormentor.

Güzin! As I sleep in this small hotel in the Transylvanian town of Bistriç, there are two points of lights shimmering near the horizon in the direction of Istanbul. Can they be your affectionate eyes?

Now I will make some notes, for I have not forgotten your interest in history:

The people of Transylvania are made up of four distinct nationalities. In the south there are the Saxons, and mixed with them the Wallachs, who are apparently the descendants of old Dacians. In the west there are the Hungarians, and in the north the Czechs. Of these I am visiting the Czechs, who claim they are the descendants of the Turkish hero Attila and the Huns who shook the world. And that is very possible, for in the 7th century when Hungarians came to these lands, they found the Huns already occupying them. According to some of the books I have read, all the primitive beliefs of the world are gathered together in this horseshoe of the Carpathian Mountains. As if this place is at the very center of a supernatural vortex. If so, the time I spend here should be very interesting. I must learn more about this from Count Dracula.

Even though my bed was quite comfortable, I still could not manage to sleep. A dog kept howling under my window all night, which may have had something to do with it. Early in the morning I arose and caught the train.

All day we traveled through a land rich with every kind of natural beauty. Sometimes we came across little towns built on steep rocks like those we see in old paintings. At every station I saw people dressed in different fashions. Some of them looked like European peasants, but some had very strange clothes. Sometimes the villagers wore absurdly wide belts with many nails—I think these are some kind of ornament. The Slovaks are the strangest-looking; they are the most primitive of the lot. It is as though they are caught between civilization and barbarism. These people pull their pants on over their long boots, let their black hair grow to their shoulders, and grow bushy moustaches. They resemble the brigands of the stage. But some of the travelers I spoke to tell me that the Slovaks are harmless folk.

The town of Bistriç is almost on the Transylvanian border. Nearby is the route to Bukovina through the mountain pass of Burgo.

In his letter, Count Dracula wrote that when I came to see him I should stop at the Golden Hotel in Bistriç. When I arrived, a stout woman in an apron, looking like a character out of a novel, appeared before me with a warm, cheery smile.

"Turk Effendi from Istanbul?" she asked.

I affirmed with a nod and sat down upon one of the sofas in the parlor downstairs. A moment later the owner of the hotel—and as far as I could tell, the husband of the stout woman—came to my side and gave me a letter. It read as follows:

"My friend!

"Welcome to the Carpathian Mountains! I have been eagerly awaiting you. Sleep well tonight at this hotel. Tomorrow afternoon at three the mail coach will leave for Bukovina. A seat has been reserved for you. At the Burgo Pass my private coach shall be waiting to bring you to me. I hope you have had a pleasant journey from Istanbul and will enjoy your stay in my beautiful country.

"Signed,
"Dracula"

Upon reading this letter, written in beautiful French, I felt some relief from my sense of alienation.

4 May.—I understood that the landlord had received a letter from Count Dracula instructing him to reserve a seat for me on the mail coach. But when I asked for particulars, he strangely pretended not to understand my German. However, this attitude could not have been genuine. Up to then he had understood my German perfectly. When I tried to ask more questions about the Count, the old man and his portly wife looked at each other as though they were afraid of something. The landlord only muttered something about the letter being sent to him with the money for the coach, and that he knew nothing else. It is very strange. Who would have thought that I would travel to such places and live as though I were in a novel?

And there is more. When I asked the landlord if he personally knew Count Dracula and Castle Dracula, they both crossed themselves in fear! It was impossible to get more from their lips than "we know nothing." Since the coach was waiting outside the hotel, I could not find the chance to ask anything further. But the landlord and his wife were acting very mysterious. The situation might appear stranger and more worrying to someone more neurotic than myself. May your ears—your tiny, pink ears ring, beautiful Güzin! If you were here now, and saw that this large woman and her husband cross themselves in fear, you would immediately think of the terrible Voivode Dracula from history. That unmatched barbarian, famed as the Impaler Voivode, who impaled thousands of Turkish captives along Danube River! That ugly and vile historical face! Do this man and his wife cross themselves when they hear the name of our client, Count Dracula, because they unconsciously recall that horrible being from the past?

There is more:

Just as I was about to leave, the landlord's old wife came into my room. Her lovely face had an anxious, hysterical look unusual for those so rotund. She came to my side and said, mysteriously:

"Will you certainly go? Oh, Turk Effendi, must you go?"

She was so anxious and worried, her broken German was getting even worse, and she was mixing in words from another language that I did not understand. I told her that I would have to go immediately, that it was my duty.

"Do you know what day this is?"

"It is the fourth of May, madam…"

"I know, I know that… I am asking do you know what day it is?"

When I told her I did not understand what she meant, she continued:

"Today is the eve of Hagia Yorgi (Saint George). Do you not know that when the clock strikes midnight, all the dark creatures and evil spirits of the world will be set free? They will have full sway. And do you not know where you are going?"

I felt an urge to laugh at this unexpected behavior and these strange words. But the poor woman was in such genuine pain and fear that the urge faded instantly. The heartfelt attention shown by this woman in a conservative, Christian country to a young Turkish man aroused in me profound feeling.

I tried to mollify her with a sober attitude. I had an

important task in front of me that needed to be taken care of, and it was impossible not to go. The evil spirits and demons of St. George's Eve would not harm good, strong-hearted people. I had given my heart to Allah. I felt nothing but love for all mankind—even demons and spirits. Therefore this poor woman had nothing to fear. The great God who created all humanity would protect us too. I said all of this to the fair and compassionate woman as clearly and convincingly as I could. I thanked her for her interest in the welfare of a stranger such as myself.

The old woman, attentive to my words, dried her teary eyes with her apron. Then, as if suddenly remembering something, she handed me a small crucifix.

I was quite taken aback by this. My position was rather awkward. Was this woman offering me the cross to kiss, or was she handing it to me so that it might protect me from the evil I may encounter? To tell the truth, I could not bring myself to kiss the piece of wood even to please this poor, decent woman. Aside from being difficult and embarrassing for a young Muslim, it was also a distasteful position for a rational man. Even a Protestant Christian, were he in my place, would hotly refuse. Nevertheless, I had a difficult time denying this poor woman. From my attitude and countenance she must have guessed what was passing through my mind, for she came even closer and placed the string of the little cross around my neck, begging me:

"For your mother's sake and for the life of your beloved!"

My dear mother had already passed away. But my beloved? Dear Güzin, you are still here. How could I refuse an offer made for your life? Ah, sweet Güzin, my angel, you should have been here and seen how this old woman baptized me with your love and the cross of Jesus. I write these lines for our personal amusement.

As I wore the cross against my chest, I thought of something: The way the woman said "for your mother's sake" was enough to recall a long-forgotten feeling. My mother was a very religious woman. When I was a child, I had swooned on several occasions; apparently I was a very nervous youth. I remember my mother dragging me to "Baba Cafer," "His Holiness Aynı Ali," and "Merkez Efendi"[1] every Friday. I had a uniquely-crafted "Enâm-ı Şerif"[2] in those days—with a beautiful, sturdy protective case—that my mother hung around my neck. I not only wore that Enâm until she died, but I carry that family heirloom with me to this day, thanks to that poor devout woman's pleading and her dying wishes. Many may laugh at me for this. It has even earned me the ridicule of my friends. But I have never gone without that heirloom my mother left to me from those lost, heavenly days of my childhood—and I never will.

When that woman hung the crucifix around my neck with her sincere and moving words, I thought about that Enâm in its little silver case. I took the Enâm, so that its rather large, amulet-shaped case showed beneath my wool scarf between my shirt and undershirt, and said to her pleasantly:

"Madam, do not worry. See, I have the holy word, the book of the great God around my neck. This will protect me."

The old woman answered:

"Very good, very good; but the crucifix will not hurt either. Keep it." And she added with unexpected solemnity and conviction: "All of them are one, all the same! All one, all one! Allah is one, everything, everyone is one… I have a young boy just like you…"

The sound of the mail coach below interrupted her speech. I earnestly shook this kind-hearted woman's hand. I hurried down the stairs to the street; I write these last lines from the coach. But it is odd… I have this strange feeling. Is it because of this country, full of demons and spirits; or because of the expression and behavior of the old landlady?

---

1   This refers to the tombs of well-known religious personages, where it is common for Muslims to pray and seek solutions to their problems.

2   A miniature extract from the Quran containing some of its most popular and important chapters, or *surahs*.

5 May. (In Dracula's Castle.)—The gray fog of the morning has passed. The sun is rising above the distant horizon. These steep hills appear to merge with the high pine trees as they reach toward the sky. After tonight's sleep on the coach I do not feel tired, so I have sat down to write in my journal until I fall asleep. I have come across many strange things that must be set down here.

When I boarded the coach at Bistriç the driver was not yet in his seat. The landlord and his wife were no doubt talking about me with the driver. I saw them turn and look at me occasionally. The pitying glances of a few layabout onlookers as they listened to the landlord and his wife made me even more uncomfortable. I was able to hear most of what was said a little distance from me. Many of these words were strange and unknown. After all, there were many nationalities in the crowd.

This unnecessary attention shown to me, combined with the earlier behavior of the landlady, greatly piqued my interest. I took my polyglot dictionary from my travel bag and began to look for the meanings of the words I could remember. Let me confess, the things I found were not at all pleasant. For example, there was "Ordoğ," meaning devil; "Pukol," meaning Hell; and "Stregoyka," meaning witch. Apart from these words, I heard "Vrolok" and "Volkoslak" which mean the same thing in Slovak; the last one meaning werewolf, vampire, or undead in Serbian. (I will try to learn more about this from Count Dracula; it is fairytale material for Güzin.)

When the coach set off, the crowd of onlookers in front of the hotel all held out their crosses and pointed two fingers at me. A few moments later I asked someone in the coach what it meant. He did not wish to answer at first, but when he understood that I was a Turk, a stranger, he explained that it was to guard against the "evil eye." For a poor outsider who was about to meet a strange man in this unknown country, this did not feel good at all. But the people around me all looked so kind, sincere, and compassionate that I could not help but feel the bittersweet sorrow in my heart begin to melt away.

Our driver cracked his long whip. The coach began to hurtle down the road. The landscape was wonderful. As I watched it, I forgot all about the hotel and everything that transpired there.

It was these valleys, forest paths, narrow passes, and rugged rocks that the moustachioed, hawk-eyed, steel-armed Turkish heroes passed with their steeds, carrying their green and red flags, battling the unknown, the barbarians, the highland nations, crushing the knights whose armor was as black as their horses as though they were crushing glass, reaching all the way up to the foggy, icy Baltic sea, thinking, "Not long to go before the Red Apple!"[3]

The road we took was steep. But the coach was traveling very fast and the driver was doing his best to go even faster. And sometimes images of Istanbul, my dear home, with its blue skies, familiar landscapes, and pretty faces under the glittering springtime sun would suddenly flash before my eyes. Then I would ask myself, "Am I dreaming?"

I understood why the driver was hurrying. He wanted to be through the famous Burgo Pass as quickly as possible. From what I had heard, this storied passage would be in fairly good condition in the summer. But at this time the rubble caused by the winter snow and floods had not yet been cleared. It is almost a historical tradition here that the roads are not kept clean and open to travel. When the Turkish sword was still sharp and Turkish rule still in place, the hospodars, princes of Erdel Transylvania, would avoid clearing and repairing the roads. For if they were repaired, the Turks would suspect the Transylvanians of calling for Polish and German allies to join forces against them, and they would break the truce and start a war.

In front of us, the dark forest ran through the high hills of the Carpathian mountain range. The afternoon sunlight created beautiful dark and light shapes where it fell over the undulating forest.

As the coach climbed the road, which wriggled like a snake

____

3   "Taking the 'Red Apple' " was a Turkish metaphor for world dominion.

beneath the hills, one of the passengers touched me and pointed out a very high snowy mountain on the horizon. He said in German, "Look, this is İsten-sezek, the seat of God," and immediately crossed himself.

Through the evening we encountered unusual-looking Czechs and Slovaks along our way. There were many crosses erected on either side of the road. As we passed them my fellow travelers all crossed themselves. It was as though they were trying to protect themselves from the coming evil.

Toward the evening the weather grew colder. As the sun set, a black fog and an icy darkness began to fall.

We started to climb toward the Burgo Pass on a steep road, through dark forests. At times we encountered places so steep that the horses had trouble pulling the coach, despite the cracking of the whip.

When darkness fell there was visible worry among the passengers. They spoke repeatedly to the driver, and they were apparently urging him to go faster. He lashed the horses mercilessly with his whip. Some time later the road ahead of us appeared to improve. Two imposing mountains on either side drew nearer the coach. We were now entering the Burgo Pass.

The passengers' worry and fidgeting had increased. They gave me strange looks and craned their heads out of the coach to look about.

We travelled along this narrow path for a while and finally came to the eastern exit of the passage.

Now I too stuck out my head, in search of the coach that I had been notified would be sent by Count Dracula. I was hoping that any moment I would see its lights in the pitch black darkness surrounding us. But there was not yet any such thing in sight.

The driver looked at his watch, then spoke a few words to the passengers in his broken German. He did it in such a low voice that I could barely hear it. I think he said that there was an hour left until the appointed time! Then he turned to me:

"Turk Effendi, as you can see there is no coach waiting for you; it seems they have forgotten. It is best if you come to

Bukovina with us tonight; you can go back tomorrow or the next day."

As he spoke, the coach's horses began to neigh and stamp. This forced the driver to tighten the reins with all his might. At the same time, the passengers made noises of fear and worry, and as they crossed themselves a four-horsed coach, known as a Kalsin, drew up next to us.

With the help of the lights on our coach, I saw that all four horses on the other were as black as coal from head to toe and were beautiful animals. The coach was driven by man with a long, black beard and a black hat with a wide brim. This wide black hat obscured his face from me completely. But as his head turned toward us, I was able see by the light of the coach a pair of crimson eyes. The man said to our driver:

"My friend, tonight you are an hour early!"

The driver tried to answer, stammering:

"The Turk Effendi was in a great hurry."

The stranger interrupted him:

"Yes, that must be why you were deceiving him, trying to take him to Bukovina. You cannot fool me, my friend. I know much more than you do, and my horses are swift!"

The newcomer smiled as he spoke these words, and the coach's lights revealed a hard-looking mouth. Its lips were a vivid red and the ivory white teeth looked extremely sharp. When the stranger finished the words, "and my horses are swift!" one of the passengers near me turned to his friend and quoted Bürger's "Lenore," whispering:

"For the dead travel fast!"

I do not know how the owner of those four horses heard this softly-recited line. But I saw him look aside with a gleaming smile, and the passenger who received the look crossed himself instantly, putting up his two fingers as I saw outside the hotel.

"Give the Effendi's luggage to me!" the stranger said. My belongings were carried quickly from our coach into the other; I descended too. Since the new carriage was already standing next to ours, the man in black held my arm to assist me. His grip was like a steel clamp. The owner of this hand must have had terrible strength. I climbed into the new coach. The stranger shook the reins without a word and the carriage turned around. We flew off into the dark abyss of the Burgo Pass.

As I looked back instinctively, I saw the horses by the lights of the old coach, steam radiating from their backs, and the passengers all crossing themselves. Then the driver cracked his long whip and called to his animals, and the mail coach started back on its way toward Bukovina.

Once my former companions were lost in the darkness of the night, a cold shiver passed through my body and a feeling of deep solitude and desolation settled in my heart. But in the intervening time, a cloak and blanket were thrown over me and the driver said in perfect German:

"Mein Herr, the nights are very cold here; my master the Count ordered me to take good care of you. There is plum rakia under the seat. You may take a few sips if you would like."

I did not touch the plum rakia, but it was a comfort to know the bottle was there. I was consumed by strange feelings; while I might have been afraid to confess it to myself, I must say that I was very frightened. If there had been any way to avoid this night journey, I would not have hesitated to take it. This trip, which I thought would be an altogether novel and pleasant experience when I left Istanbul, was taking a turn for the worse.

After traveling for some time, the coach suddenly made a complete turn and began down a different road. It appeared to me that we were going over the same ground over and over. Once I suspected that this was the case, I took note of some salient points and confirmed my suspicions. I thought for a moment about asking the man why he was doing this, but I abandoned the idea. If it was intended to delay my arrival to the Count, my protest would be useless. By-and-by, as I was curious what time it was, I struck a match and looked at my watch.

It was a few minutes to midnight…

This gave me an unexpected shock. The things I had seen in the last few hours had given a weird potency to the primitive and terrifying superstitions of these ignorant people, and especially the villagers' fears about midnight. With an anxiety that nearly caused me to faint, I waited.

Suddenly a dog began to howl far away, perhaps from a farmhouse on the other side of the road. The howl was a long and agonizing wail, uttered as if in great fear. It was followed by another one, and then another dog howled! And another dog! And one more! This wild, heartbreaking wailing was borne on the wind, blowing like a deep, slow moan through the Burgo Pass. It was as if the sound was enveloping the entire area, and even the whole country, in a deep, terrible darkness. At the first howl, the horses started and began to turn back. When the driver spoke soothingly to the animals they recovered, but I could see them sweat and shake. Then, far off in the distance, from the mountains on each side of us began a louder and a sharper howling—that of wolves. These new howls had the same frightening effect on both the horses and myself. For not only did I have a mind to jump from the calèche and flee, but the horses also began to rear up, move back, and struggle to get away from the coach. The driver had to use all of his strength on the reins. Eventually my ears grew accustomed to the howling. The animals too began to calm down. The driver got out of his seat and approached the horses. He stroked and talked to them. And although they still trembled, they did begin to return to their senses.

The driver again took his seat and shook the reins. We started off at a great pace. This time, after reaching the far side of the Burgo Pass we suddenly took a sharp right turn down a narrow path. We passed through dense forest and entered a steep mountain passage enclosing us on either side. The wind blew powerfully around us and the trees shook as though they were about to topple. The cold intensified and finally a dusty snow began to fall. A few moments later, everything was covered in a white shroud of snow. A sharp wind still carried the howls of the dogs to us, but as we moved further away these sounds grew fainter. However, the baying of the wolves increased steadily as though they had surrounded us and were closing in. I grew afraid, and the horses shared my fear. But strangely the driver was not at all disturbed. He constantly turned his head left and right; but I was unable to see anything in the pitch black darkness that surrounded us.

Suddenly, away on our left, I saw a bright flame; the driver had seen it too. He stopped the horses immediately, jumped down, and faded into the darkness. I do not know what he did there, but the howling of the wolves grew closer; that much was certain. While I waited in terror and anticipation, the driver suddenly returned and took his seat without saying a word; we began moving again.

I think now that I had fallen asleep by the time these maddening events took place and that I was actually seeing them in my dreams. Because as I write these lines, they seem like a terrible nightmare.

Once in particular that blue flame I mentioned shone so close to the road that by its light I was able to see what the coachman did. He went rapidly toward the light once more and, gathering a few stones, formed them into some sign.

I observed a very strange illusion. Although the driver was standing between myself and the blue flame, the fire was still visible. The driver's torso did not obstruct my view of the light. This caused me nearly to jump from my seat. But as it only lasted a few seconds I ascribed it to the weariness of my eyes, straining through the darkness for so long. Finally there came a time when the driver stopped the coach and went even further than before; while he was gone the horses began to stamp, rear up, and tremble uncontrollably. I could not understand why, for the howling of the wolves had ceased altogether. Then, at that very moment, the moon emerged briefly from behind the dark clouds and illuminated the area.

My God! We were surrounded by a sea of wolves! In front of us, at our back, and all around us were wolves with lolling crimson red tongues, white teeth, and shaggy manes and fur.

When these monsters howled, looking like that, they were a hundred times more terrifying. Seeing them so, I was paralyzed with fear. There is no way for a man to fully understand such a horror without experiencing it for himself.

Suddenly the wolves began howling all together, as though the moonlight had a peculiar effect on them. I shouted to the coachman to return. At that moment I heard a voice and looked in its direction. Lo and behold! The driver, whom I thought was beyond the pack of wolves, had inexplicably appeared in the middle of the road. As he opened his arms in a gesture of command, the wolves retreated timorously.

When dense clouds obscured the face of the moon once more, complete darkness fell.

When I could see my surroundings again, I saw the driver climbing into his seat—and the wolves had disappeared!

This was so strange, horrifying, and surreal, a mass of gnawing fear assailed my senses; it was impossible to speak or move. As we continued on our way through this sea of darkness, it was as though time had come to a stop. I seemed to be living through long, torturous centuries!

The coach steadily ascended the hills.

Suddenly I became aware that the coachman was pulling his horses into the courtyard of a vast ruined castle. There was no light emanating from its black windows, and the broken towers and battlements of the large cluster of buildings showed a jagged line against the starlit sky.

CHAPTER II

5 May.—I must have fallen asleep the last few minutes in the coach. For had I been awake I would surely have noticed the approach of such a remarkable place. The courtyard of the castle looked exceptionally large compared with the surrounding emptiness. Three or four roads running under high arches also contributed to its expansive and somber appearance.

When the coach stopped, the driver jumped from his seat and reached out to help me alight. That was when I realized once again how terribly strong this man was. His hand was just like a steel vice. He could have crushed mine with one grasp if he had wished.

As I stood in front of a large, sturdy door studded with nails, he unloaded my traps one by one. Then he quickly got into his seat and shook the reins, and suddenly the horses, driver, and coach vanished into the darkness.

I waited as though frozen in place, for there was no bell or knob on this door, which had evidently borne witness to centuries. There was no way that any sound I could make would have made it through those ominous windows or thick walls. The waiting seemed endless; hundreds of disturbing thoughts and gnawing fears ran rampant in my head.

Oh, what troubled place was I visiting, and to see what kind of people? How could I have blindly thrown myself into this adventure?

What resemblance was there between an ordinary lawyer, traveling to another country to deliver official documents and bills, provide necessary legal information, and give counsel to a stranger who has bought a property in Istanbul; and myself, who has endured the events of last night and today?

Ah, dear Güzin, how happy we were when the manager of my office, the honorable Rıfat Bey, assigned me to this job. Of course I was still in my apprenticeship as an assistant attorney when I was given the assignment, which amounted to a sudden promotion. A budding new lawyer, a businessman! Soon we will be able to be married. Even though we have very little money at present, we shall move forward with our dream of starting a family, planning our future, and becoming prosperous. My dear Güzin, these are all your words, and the sweet voice of your joyous soul rings in my ears even now.

I began to rub my eyes and pinch myself to see if I were dreaming. This all seemed like a terrible delusion to me. I hoped that I would open my eyes and find myself lying on my bed near the window, listening to the sweet sounds of Turkish carried in from the streets. But I had no doubt that I was awake. I was not wrong. I was awake, far from my motherland, beautiful Istanbul—spring-like, radiant, full of love—and in a wild, unknown corner of the Carpathians, in a fount of darkness and fear.

As these thoughts passed through my mind, footsteps approached the thick door from the other side and a light appeared through the keyhole. Chains rattled; huge rusted bolts moved from their places with a terrible noise; a large key turned inside a lock which apparently had not been used for some time, and the massive door opened inwards.

A tall, old man stood in front of it. He had a long white mustache and no beard. He was dressed in black from head to toe. There was not even a hint of another color on the man.

He held a silver, almost antique candlestick in his hand with nothing to protect the flame that flickered in the draught. The old man made a graceful, inviting gesture with his right hand, and with excellent Turkish but a strange accent he said:

"Welcome to my home. Please enter freely and of your own accord without hesitation!"

Hearing such good Turkish in this place and under these circumstances completely bewildered me. His accent resembled that of some of the Greek doctors in Istanbul.

When he took my hand and shook it, his strength was just like that harsh strength of the driver who brought me here—so much so that I suspected they were the same person. Apart from that, his hand, gripping mine as though it were about to break my bones, was as cold as ice and resembled that of a dead man.

To ease my confusion I asked:

"Do I have the honor of addressing Count Dracula?"

He bowed with great courtesy and grace:

"Yes, I am Dracula. And I am pleased to bid the lawyer Azmi Bey welcome to my castle."

As he spoke these words in accented Turkish, the tall old man placed the candlestick on a stone. He stepped out and brought my bags inside; I objected to his taking the trouble and offered to help. He responded again in Turkish:

"Nay sir, not at all. It is very late, and my servants are not here; please let me see to your comfort myself!"

He brought the bags and trunks to a spiral staircase. After climbing the steps, we passed through a long hallway. The Count's footsteps rang heavily in this stone passage. The Count opened a strong, heavy door at the end of the corridor. We entered a large, well-lit room. There was a round table with food set upon it and a cozy, roaring hearth visible on the other side of the room.

Count Dracula stopped, setting my bags and trunks to the side. He then opened another door, where there was a smaller, octagonal room illuminated by a single lamp. This small room had no windows. We passed through this room as well.

The Count opened a third door and motioned for me to enter. Before me was a very welcome sight, for this was a well-lit bedroom heated with a large fireplace. The giant logs in the hearth burned with pleasant crackling sounds and vented their smoke up the wide chimney. Count Dracula brought my belongings in here, left them inside the door, and said:

"After such a long journey you must surely wish to change your clothes, rest, and put your belongings in place. Here you will find everything you need. When you are ready, come into the parlor; your supper is already prepared."

The Count quickly withdrew. The bright, warm environment in which I found myself and the kind, courteous behavior of Count Dracula had immediately dissipated all my fears and suspicions. Having then reached my natural state, I discovered that I was starving. I hastily prepared myself and went into the parlor.

Just as he said, the supper was laid out on the table. Standing next to a carved statue near the large fireplace, my host invited me to the table with a respectful and graceful gesture.

"Please, be seated and sup how you please. I ask your forgiveness because I cannot join you; I have dined a little early today and it is not my habit to eat at night."

I handed Count Dracula the letter, sealed with red wax, written by Rıfat Bey, the director of my office in Istanbul. Count Dracula opened the envelope, read the letter solemnly, and then, with a smile, gave it back to me to read. As I perused this letter from Rıfat Bey, who is as dear to me as my father, I think some lines made me blush with happiness. I felt a deep sense of gratitude toward Rıfat Bey, and a strong feeling of pride. Referring to his recent rheumatism, Rıfat Bey wrote:

"...As such, this unfortunate illness prevents me from making this journey. But I am happy to say that I can send a highly trusted attorney of mine in my stead. He may appear very young, but he is highly energetic, cultured, enlightened, and honest. He is discreet and knows how to hold his tongue. I would like to add that he was raised under my patronage and careful supervision, and thereafter completed his education and training. Azmi Bey, my attorney and second son, will stay there as long as you wish after giving you the necessary information. He will acquaint you with the property we purchased for you in Istanbul, through our correspondence, with your permission and under your name. I am deeply sorry that I could not make this trip myself to meet you in person…"

After I finished the letter, the Count approached the table and removed the cover of a dish; a salad and the famous Hungarian Tokaji wine, with which I was only familiar through novels, complemented the supper. I made a point to drain two glasses of the wine. Count Dracula asked me many questions about my trip and I told him everything that had happened to me. I could not wait to ask many questions myself.

When the supper was over, I drew up a chair near the fire and began to smoke the cigarettes the Count offered me. Count Dracula said that he did not smoke, and apologized.

I now had the chance to observe my host closely. The Count's face and appearance struck me as remarkable. His face was strong, very strong, and his profile was aquiline. His slim nose had a high bridge and his nostrils were arched. His forehead was lofty, so much so as to indicate nobility. His hair, which was thin at the temples, was thick and bushy elsewhere. His eyebrows were also bushy and furrowed, and they nearly conjoined above his nose. As far as I could see under his heavy, white moustache, his mouth suggested great and almost merciless determination. The teeth were strangely sharp and very pointed. And his lips were a blood-red color unusual for a man of his age; they showed an astonishing vitality. His ears were rather pale and the tops were excessively pointed. His jaw was broad and strong, and his cheeks, while thin, still appeared firm. The general impression of his face was one of exceptional pallor.

Until now I had only seen my host's hands by the light of the fireplace, and they appeared white and delicate. But now I could see that there were hairs in the center of his palm. Beyond this, his hands and coarse fingers were long and thin and his fingernails were pointed.

As the Count leaned toward me and touched my hand, a shudder passed through my body. Moreover, the man's breath was rank, worse than any other. It caused at that moment a wave of nausea to come over me and I was unable to conceal it. Count Dracula undoubtedly sensed this and stepped back. With a grim smile that displayed his long, sharp teeth even more, he moved back to the other side of the roaring fireplace and sat down.

For a while we were both silent. And at that moment, my eyes discerned the first shimmering rays of sunlight through the windows. There was a strange stillness. But suddenly I heard many wolves howling from the deep valleys down below. His eyes shining, the Count said:

"Listen to them… Children of the night! What a beautiful symphony they play!"

He added, upon seeing my reaction:

"Ah, you city dwellers, you can never understand the life of a hunter…"

Then he rose suddenly:

"Effendi from Istanbul, you must be very tired from your journey. Your bedroom is ready; tomorrow you may sleep as late as you wish. I have other business until the evening. Now make yourself comfortable, and dream well!"

Then he opened the door of the octagonal room with a graceful bow. I entered my bedroom. As the old Turkish poets put it, I was in a sea of bewilderment. And I had delved into a vortex of curiosity. I was suspicious and frightened. I think things that I am afraid to admit even to myself. May God help me. Güzin, dear Güzin, do you see your poor Azmi in your dreams as you sleep this morning in our sweet Istanbul?

7 May.—Morning again. I have been very comfortable during the last twenty-four hours. I slept until late in the morning and woke of my own accord. When I had dressed, I went to the parlor where I had had supper, and there was a cold breakfast on the table and a hot coffeepot near the fireplace. There was a card on the table, upon which was written in German:

"I will not be in the castle for a while. Please do not wait for me.

"Signed, COUNT DRACULA"

After reading the card I sat down to table and had a large breakfast. After I finished my meal, I looked for a bell to call a servant to clear the plates, but I could not find one. From what I have seen there are some strange deficiencies in the castle and in my room. These seem especially odd when compared with the evidences of great wealth. For example, the cutlery is of gold. It is so well-made that it is doubtless of great value. The curtains, carpets, and bed sheets are all fashioned from the heaviest and most costly fabric. Although they were made hundreds of years ago, they are yet undamaged. But in none of the rooms is there a single mirror! I could not even find a vanity mirror over my table, so I took out the small mirror in my shaving box so that I might shave and smarten myself up. Not only have I seen no servants inside the castle, but I have not heard any noise apart from the howling wolves. I ate my breakfast; to be honest I do not know if I should call it a breakfast or dinner, for it was about five or six o'clock when I had eaten. I looked around to find something to read, since I did not think it was appropriate to go about the castle without the Count's permission. There was nothing resembling a book, paper, or ink; eventually, I found some kind of library when I opened the other door. I checked the door of the room opposite mine, but it was locked.

After I entered the library I was both surprised and overjoyed, as there were many, indeed an indescribable number, of Turkish books! Many shelves were full of them. The Count had certainly been to Istanbul, since he knew Turkish, so seeing some Turkish books here should not have come as a surprise. But they were so many and varied that I began to wonder if Count Dracula was an orientalist interested in the language, culture, and history of eastern nations, like Vambery. This was plausible. The reason he communicated with our bureau in Istanbul, sent a deed of trust to our director Rıfat Bey, and purchased a house in Istanbul was to more closely conduct his research and observations. There were bound Turkish newspapers and magazines everywhere. Many of these were from twenty, thirty years ago.

As for the subjects of these Turkish books, there was a wide variety. There were books about history, geography, politics, law, many novels, and even a newly printed book on etiquette. Strangely, there were even trade registries and bound copies of the Istanbul Chamber of Commerce's periodical. When I saw the journal of the Turkish Bar Association, I had the sweet sensation of seeing a close relative.

Whilst I was looking at these books, the door suddenly opened and Count Dracula entered. After greeting me cheerfully and asking how I was getting along, he said:

"I am glad you found the library, for there are many things that will interest you here."

And then he put his hands on one of the Turkish history books:

"These are my sweet-voiced friends. I have spent my years with them. In particular, ever since I decided to visit Istanbul I have made good use of them. From them I learned the history and the beauty of Turkey. And I have even loved it. How I long to wander the crowded streets of Istanbul, the center of the world and its history, queen of the eastern world and a diamond among cities. But unfortunately all the Turkish I know I have taught myself from books. I trust to your friendship and your help with this."

I answered with surprise:

"But Count, you speak Turkish very well! Indeed I thought you had been in Turkey for a long time."

"Thank you for your compliment, Turk Effendi. But I recognize I have much to learn. Yes, I know the grammar and the words well. But I lack practice."

I said again, "Count, you speak exceptionally well."

He laughed.

"Yes, I do; hence I shall have no difficulty when I come to

Istanbul. I can even manage much of my business myself. But Azmi Bey, this is not enough for me. I am one of the nobles of my country; I am a Boyar. Everyone here knows me; I am their master. They will respect me regardless. But this is not the case in a foreign country; there, nobody really cares about a stranger. If you make a mistake in grammar or in accent they will say, 'Look at how this stranger speaks Turkish!' and laugh at you to your face. I cannot bear that. I have been my own master for so long, I cannot accept the idea of someone else being master of me or laughing at me. Therefore you do not come here merely as the attorney of the business management director, Rıfat Bey, but you shall also sit here and help me with my pronunciation errors in Turkish! You may roam this castle however you like, but I hope you will wish to stay away from closed or locked doors."

And then we began to speak Turkish at the Count's request. For a while I talked about the things I saw when I traveled here in the coach. He evaded some of my questions with skillful wordplay, and answered others in an easy manner:

"Azmi Bey, remember, you are in Transylvania, known as Erdel in your history. This place is nothing like your country. Its traditions and beliefs are different. According to local superstition, for example, on one night of the year—the night you came—it is believed that all demons and witches are set free; and blue flames are seen in places where treasure has been concealed. It is probable that there were some hidden treasures in the places you passed in my coach. For your armies fought many bloody battles with the Wallachians and Saxons here, and the people of Transylvania used to bury their valuables in remote places like this. But those with the courage to mark the locations of these blue flames may find them the next day."

And then the Count said:

"Now, Azmi Bey, my friend, tell me about the house you procured in Istanbul."

I arose from my seat, went to my room, and retrieved the necessary papers concerning the business. When I came back into the library, everything had been cleared; on the table was a large-scale block plan of Istanbul, printed by the Istanbul city council some time ago. The fact that the Count placed this much importance on everything was surprising. I began to describe in detail the purchased house, and to my great surprise I found that the Count knew the neighborhoods of Istanbul, particularly the one in which the mansion is situated, almost better than myself! Finally all the necessary facts were given, the Count signed some papers, and a letter was written to my director, Rıfat Bey.

The mansion we procured for Count Dracula was in a neighborhood matching his stated requirements and of the type he requested. Count Dracula desired a building reminiscent of the Turkish spirit, with a large garden and in a quiet area. And he had written that no expense should be spared. Apparently he wished to live in a place known for its historical significance, full of old life and poetry, like the famous French writer and old Istanbul enthusiast Pierre Loti. The mansion we purchased was the remains of an old public building outside Eyüp and was, according to the locals, scheduled to be demolished. In a far corner of its garden there were such buildings as a stable, servants' quarters, and a mausoleum.

The Count was very pleased with this description. Presently, with an excuse, Count Dracula left the library. As I looked at the Istanbul map in front of me, I observed some circles drawn in pencil around certain neighborhoods; one of those markings was just over the area of Eyüp where we purchased the mansion. In addition, there were circles around Bakırköy, Şişli, and Sarıyer. Did this man want, or had he already bought, property in these areas as well?

After about half an hour, the Count returned.

"Ohhh," he said, "you are still busy with the books, it seems. But this is too much work. Please come, they have informed me that your supper is ready."

He took my arm and we went out. An excellent table was set in the parlor. Count Dracula again told me that he was not hungry and apologized for not joining me. I sat down to table alone; while I ate, he chatted and asked me questions. After dinner, although it felt very late I said nothing. Because I had gotten plenty of sleep, I did not feel tired.

Finally, the crow of a rooster was heard through the chill of the morning, and suddenly Count Dracula leapt from his chair and said:

"Oh, I have kept you up all night again. You are such good company, I did not notice the passage of time."

And he left the room with a graceful bow.

8 May.—When I began this journal I was worried about going into too many specifics, but now I am happy that I have discussed every event in detail. I am witnessing and experiencing so many strange phenomena that it is impossible not to feel afraid. Ah, if only I could be safely out of here. Or had never come here in the first place! Perhaps sitting up every night until the morning has made me lose my nerve. But if only that were all… If I could find a friend to talk to, I could put up with this. However, it is impossible! The only one I can speak to is Count Dracula. But the Count, this man…

Oh, I am frightened. Could I be the only living soul in this castle?

When I went to bed I could not manage to sleep, so after tossing and turning for a while, I rose. I had hung my small shaving mirror beside the window, and to make use of my free time I had begun to shave, when suddenly I saw a hand touching my shoulder and heard the Count say:

"Good morning!"

I was greatly startled, for although the mirror in front of me displayed the entire room, I could not see Count Dracula in it! When I turned my head toward him in astonishment, I cut my face with the razor, though I did not notice it. After greeting the Count, I turned to the mirror once again to see if I had been mistaken. This time there could be no possibility that I was wrong; for the Count was standing right behind me and I was able to see over my shoulder. But there was still no reflection in the mirror! The area of the room behind me was visible, but there was no sign of any other man in the mirror except myself.

This was really an alarming occurrence. Combined with the other extraordinary things I had encountered, it exacerbated the feeling of uneasiness I had whenever the Count was around me. As I continued shaving, these thoughts in my mind, I saw that the razor cut was bleeding and that blood had dripped from my chin to my shirt. I turned back toward the Count, searching for something to wipe away the blood. When Count saw my bleeding face, his eyes began to blaze with a demonic violence and passion. He touched the string of my mother's Enâm case, and his facial expression changed suddenly. That evil passion faded so quickly, I could not believe what I had just seen.

The Count:

"Be careful, please be careful not to cut your face; such things are very dangerous in our country!" said the Count, and taking my shaving mirror from in front of me he continued:

"Here is the thing that caused you this trouble. Let us throw this filthy thing away!" And with his tremendously strong hands he opened a large window and flung my mirror from it. Then he stormed out of the room.

When I went into the dining room the table was ready and I had my breakfast. It is strange, but I have never seen the Count eat anything, or drink water or wine! After breakfast I decided to explore the castle. I found a room with windows facing south. The castle was just on the edge of a very dangerous and terrible cliff. A stone thrown here could fall a thousand meters without hitting anything. The view was of a range of pine trees. The scene was quite beautiful and relaxing, but at the moment I am in no mood to talk about beauty or relaxation. For after exploring the castle a little further, I realized that many of the very large and heavy doors I came across in every direction were locked, and that there was no exit to the outside except from the castle's windows.

The castle is like a giant, terrible prison…

And I am the prisoner!

CHAPTER III

When I realized I was nothing but a prisoner in the castle, I felt a maddening fear and a rush of insanity. I went up and down all the stairs and tried to peer from every window and door. But a few moments later, exhaustion and despair overpowered my other feelings. When I recall that state of mind a few hours later, I think that I had gone completely mad; but when I became convinced that escape was impossible, I strangely regained my sense of calm. I took shelter in my room. I began coolly to consider what to do. I am thinking still. But it is impossible to reach a conclusion. One thing is absolutely clear: I will not tell the Count what I am thinking; it is no use. He knows better than I do that I am trapped. If I say that he is the one keeping me locked in here and that there is surely a motive behind it, he would try to deceive me. The only thing I can do is keep my thoughts to myself and stay alert and vigilant. I know that I am either deceived by my own imaginary fears, like an infant, or I am in terrible, desperate straits!

Just as I was thinking these things, I heard the large door close downstairs, and I knew that Count Dracula had returned. Since he did not come to the library where I was, I went to my bedroom and saw the Count there, making my bed himself. This was strange. But my suspicions were confirmed by what I saw. There is no servant of any kind in the castle. This new thought gave me a fright; it meant that the strange driver who brought me in the coach to the castle was none other than the Count himself. This was a terrible thought! With what kind of evil strength had this man effortlessly subdued thousands of wild wolves on that hellish night? What made the people of Bistriç give me looks of intense pity, fear, and reticence as though I were a sheep headed for the slaughter? Apart from the crucifix the landlady gave me, had not the innocent villagers I accompanied on the trip given me strange gifts like garlic and wild rose? Now that I remembered the cross the landlady gave to me, I put my hand in my pocket. It was still there; I could not bring myself to throw away that woman's precious keepsake. But amid the wild thoughts filling my head, the crucifix recalled to me the miniature Enâm on my neck, with its significance to me because of my dear departed mother's will. Oh, how strange. Now I put my hand on my chest and felt the small, exquisitely crafted case under my shirt. It gave me a sense of unimaginable strength and comfort. The smiling face of my dear, pure, devout mother flashed before my eyes in a cluster of light. I am not an unbeliever; but to a man who has been indifferent to his religious duties, the feeling of strength and comfort from the presence and contact of an Enâm was really astonishing. I will try to force Count Dracula to talk about himself tonight.

Midnight.—I have had a long conversation with the Count. I have asked him some questions and he is remarkably interested in my nation's history, in those brave Turkish armies and Turkish raiders, in the old Turkish political ideas, and in the history of this country, Erdel—that is, Transylvania. He answered my queries with surprising knowledge and vividness, even for a Transylvanian. As he talked of this country's history, and in particular its wars, he spoke with rage, strength, and enthusiasm, as though he had been personally involved in the events. But I also noticed how he restrained himself and tried to give a milder tone to his words and behavior. He specifically wished to bypass or gloss over events centered around the Turkish Empire. This seemed only natural; could he behave otherwise with a Turk? He would not have felt it appropriate to vaunt or glorify his namesake, who perpetrated terrible, bloody cruelties and tortures on Turks; who broke his oath, his word of honor many times and earned such sinister nicknames as Devil Voivode and Impaler Voivode, even if the man is a hero of sorts for Transylvanians. But because of this I realized a fact that provoked in me perhaps undue and excessive resentment and disgust. Was not the man who employs me, whose castle I have slept in, whose bread I have eaten, and who stands before me today, Count Dracula of Transylvania? A descendant of that historical, merciless, cruel Wallachian Prince Dracula, the Impaler Voivode! And even this ruined castle, where eagles would fear to nest, is a remnant from the Impaler Voivode's time, and one of his last remaining strongholds. Ah, my dear, sweet historian Güzin, how I long to see you now. If you were here, who knows what you might feel and say about this coincidence—of a similar name turning out to be a lineage, a family. I wish I could write down everything the Count said during this conversation. But in addition to the worries already in my mind, I was so shocked by this coincidence that the experience of tonight gave the impression of a bad dream, a nightmare. For now I was under the roof of a castle which once sheltered the Impaler Voivode. How many times did he hide in this remote castle to escape the avenging sword of Turkish raiders, his hands still stained with the blood of innocent, unarmed Turkish women and children whom he had killed, impaled, and nailed on the head? Perhaps he threw the last of his Turkish captives into that dark, desolate courtyard—or even tortured them to death right outside this room!

Although the Count attempted to appear calm, as he grew excited he wandered around the room, pulling at his long white moustache almost aggressively and grasping whatever he came across as though he wished to crush it. I shall put down some of the things he said in those unbalanced, excited moments:

"We Szekelys have the right to be a proud people, for the blood of a heroic race flows through our veins! The bravest fighters from the north and west of Europe were halted here. They could not pass this region, for those nations found the Huns, the Huns of great Attila here. Those Huns, with their bravery and fury, swept the whole world with a storm of fire. They spelled the doom of other nations. The defeated, ignorant peoples believed that these heroes were descended from a race which, exiled from Turkestan, had bred with devils in the deserts. Fools, nitwits! What devil, what spirit, what wizard has been created that was as fierce, as brave, and as illustrious as great Attila? Turk Effendi, you get your share of my praise too. This Attila, these Huns whose blood I am proud to carry in my veins, are your ancestors too. That is why we Szekelys were entrusted with the protection of the border between Hungary and Turkey. These two sister nations fought for centuries with heroic ideals, and both sides washed the mountains and rivers with their blood. Was it not the brave Dracula who crossed the Danube River to fight the terrible Turkish armies, after tasting defeat on the bloody plains of Kosovo, to clear this shame and disgrace from my ancestors? Such a shame that his treacherous brother sold this country to you, and my people bore the yoke of enslavement under the Turkish sword. They say that great Dracula was a traitor and abandoned his soldiers when he was defeated. Bah, what importance do such things have? A few thousand peasants without a leader are nothing. If Dracula made it out alive, the war could begin again. But if he had died, all would have been over…"

The Count suddenly came to his senses and lapsed into silence. Forcing a smile, he said quietly:

"Oh Azmi Bey, I waste time abandoning myself to these memories of the past; they are now only sweet, thrilling illusions!"

By this time it was close on morning. We parted company.

(I have noticed that my diary looks a great deal like "A Thousand and One Nights" or the ghostly visits of Hamlet's father, always beginning in the evening. And ending when the rooster crows...)

12 May.[4]—Tonight the Count asked me questions about legal matters in Turkey. For instance whether he could, in writing, authorize multiple individuals to handle various matters on his behalf in Istanbul. This was followed by questions about business management, freight companies, and shipping agents in Istanbul.

For example, he had obtained the addresses of some shipping companies who could deliver to specific addresses or destinations in Istanbul by ferry. Their addresses and advertisements were already in the books and catalogues in the library. And the Count's knowledge of such matters, as well as the workings of our ports, was exceptional.

Presently he asked, indifferently:

"Have you written to your director Rıfat Bey or anyone else?

When I answered, "No!" he put his hand on my shoulder: "If that is so, my friend, then you must write to my friend Rıfat Bey by name and tell him that you shall stay here with me for another month to complete the job."

My heart felt gripped by a claw of ice. I could not help myself and asked:

"Will I stay so long?"

"I desire it much; let me even say that I will take no excuses. Did not your director Rıfat Bey say that you are responsible for handling my difficult affairs here?"

What could I say to this? Apart from everything else, this job had been given to me by my director, and in a way my patron, Rıfat Bey. How could I let childish fears disrupt all this work? And there was something about Count Dracula's words

---

4   The Turkish adaptation contains no date here. However, as the entry indicates a new day, and because Stoker's original text includes the date, for the sake of clarity the date has been reinstated.

which reminded me that I was already a prisoner here.

Then he took out three sheets of notepaper and three envelopes from his pockets and handed them to me. On them I wrote two letters: one to Rıfat Bey and the other to my dear fiancée Güzin. In that time the Count wrote two or three letters in French, referring to some books on his desk. When I finished, he took my two letters from the desk and went into another room, presumably to take care of other business. During this time, I swiftly looked at the addresses of the other letters. One of these was written to an employment agency in Istanbul and the other was to a freight company. Presently Count Dracula returned, and after picking up these letters he said:

"I trust you will forgive me, but I have much business that I must take care of tonight."

Having said this, he walked to the door; but then he suddenly stopped and added these words:

"I must explain something very important: if you leave these rooms, never fall asleep in any other part of the castle. For this ruined castle has been the scene of many great events, and there are bad dreams for those who choose their sleeping places unwisely. Should you feel tired somewhere else, return to your bedroom or here immediately!"

The Count left and I was lost in thought. Could there be a worse, more terrifying nightmare than this supernatural darkness that has been closing in around me?

One or two hours later.—Oh, I would prefer to sleep anywhere but in the presence of Count Dracula!

After the Count left, I went to my bedroom. After a time, I came out again. I went up the stone stair where I could look out to the south. Although I had no chance of reaching the expanse below, seeing it provided some relief. I was already on edge; although I tried to give myself courage, dark clouds were settling inside my mind. As I looked through the window, the moonlight illuminated the scene as though it were daytime. I leaned out to get a better look around when my eye caught something strange, moving slowly, a story below me.

What I saw was the head of Count Dracula leaning out from the window. I stepped back and watched. At first this did not seem of particular interest. But a few moments later my feelings changed to terror and confusion when I saw the Count completely emerge from the window and climb, like a lizard, down the outer wall of the castle above that steep, dark cliff. I absolutely could not believe my eyes. But there he was, Count Dracula. He was moving downward, grasping the irregular protrusions of the wall with his fingers.

What kind of a man, or creature in human form, is this?

Oh… I feel the dread of this castle overpowering me. I am frightened; there is absolutely no escape from here. I am trembling, face to face with fears of which I dare not even think…

15 May.—Once more I have seen the Count crawling down the wall like a lizard. He moved down and to the left for about a hundred feet and then vanished into some sort of hole or window. When I realized the Count had left the castle, I decided to take advantage of this opportunity and explore. I went to my room and, taking a candle, began trying all the doors I encountered. All of them were locked, and the locks were incongruously new compared to the doors themselves. I went down to the courtyard where I had first entered the castle and the large door there was locked as well. The key was certainly in the Count's room. To open that great door, or to find it open, would be the most reasonable route to escape. Afterward, I tried some of the other doors; all of them were locked, but I was able to force one which communicated with another wing, and I entered this new area of the castle. There were many rooms here. The moonlight poured in through the wide, curtainless windows, filling the room and rendering the candle in my hand almost useless. But I was glad that I had it, for there was a terrible desolation and unnatural silence all around me. Still, it seemed far better to me than my own room, which I had greatly come to hate and fear from the presence of the Count. I tried for a while to calm my nerves and felt a soft quietude come over me. I write these lines of my journal from here.

16 May, morning.—Great God, spare me from going insane! For to this I am reduced. There is no longer any assurance of peace, safety, or escape. All I can hope for is that I may not go mad. Have I gone mad already? Oh god, what have I become? Now think: This sinister castle is terrifying, so full of dark and vile things that the Count appears the least foul and dreadful among them! From these maddening, shadowy dangers I am now compelled to look to the Count for safety, even if it is only for so long as I serve his purpose.

Oh, great God, merciful and almighty God!

Let me try to be calm. For if I do not I must surely go insane. I shall pour my misery into this diary as has been my habit since childhood. It gives me some comfort to write down my grief.

The Count warned me never to sleep in any of the other rooms, but I paid this little heed. After roaming the other side of the castle and writing about it at a desk I discovered there, I put my notebook and pencil in my pocket. I began to feel sleepy. Although the Count's warning crossed my mind, the moonlight streaming in through the window and the spectacular scenery persuaded me to sleep here. I lay down on the dusty sofa in front of the window. I think I fell asleep instantly. But what followed was so vivid, so real and substantial, that as I write these lines in daylight I cannot believe that I was sleeping. Let me explain:

I was not alone in that room in which I had fallen asleep. Judging by their dress and manner, there were three young women or girls in the room. But strangely, although they stood beneath the moonlight, they threw no shadows on the floor. These three girls came over to me, looked at me for some time, and whispered to each other. Two of them were dark beauties. Their faces resembled that of the Count. The third was fair-haired and also exceptionally beautiful. Their eyes gleamed red in the moonlight. All three of them had brilliant white teeth. These shone under cherry-red lips flush with sensuality and passion. These girls had a strange aura, and there was something about them which both attracted me and instilled in me an icy fear. I felt a strong, wicked desire deep in my heart for these girls to come and kiss me with their fiery, red lips! My dear Güzin, I should not write these things here, for perhaps one day you will read these lines and they will cause you pain; but I cannot help it, it is the truth!

They whispered, and then the three girls burst into laughter. This laughter was sweet, yet also rough and harsh, clawing at my heart. The two brunettes were urging the fair-haired girl to do something. One of them said:

"Go ahead, it is your turn; go kiss him! See, he is young and strong. He has strength enough to be kissed by all of us."

The fair-haired girl moved forward and bent over me; I felt her breath on my face. Here I felt a faint thrill and a dull sickening sensation at the same time. I detected a foul odor, like blood. I watched, under my eyelashes, as the girl knelt down. Her face trembled, as though with intense thirst, and she licked her lips like an animal. Her crimson tongue was visible between her sharp, white teeth. That beautiful head leaned down even further. I felt a warmth on my neck and two sharp teeth touched my skin. I was in the agonizing grip of a strange, painful ecstasy—overwhelmed!

But just at that moment another sensation swept over me. From beneath my eyelashes I saw the Count approaching with a dark, furious countenance that seemed enveloped in a black cloud. With his strong hands he grasped the girl who knelt over me by her white, delicate neck. Although she displayed intense rage at this interference, he hurled that exquisite face behind him as though she were a feather, and then motioned imperiously for them to back away; this was the same command that had been given to the wolves when I traveled to the castle! The Count's voice sounded like a snake's hiss.

"How dare you?" he said. "How dare you touch a man who belongs to me? Have I not forbidden you to touch?"

Then he continued in a calm, soft voice:

"Do not be angry, your time will come; you shall kiss him also. After I am finished with him. Now leave, for there is work that I must make him do."

Then one of the girls pointed to a large bag which the Count had thrown upon the floor as he entered, and which appeared to have something alive within it.

"So tonight we have nothing but this?" she asked.

Count Dracula nodded his head yes; one of the girls leapt upon the bag with the passion of a hyena and opened it. If my ears did not deceive me, I heard the wail of a child from the bag.

I turned away in infinite horror as the girls knelt down around the bag and ran off with it. But they did not pass through the door; they simply faded into the cold moonlight. Presently, I must have completely blacked out.

CHAPTER IV

FROM AZMİ BEY'S DIARY—*continued*

When I awoke I found myself in my room and in my bed. If everything I had seen was not a nightmare, then the Count himself must have brought me here from that terrible room. My clothes had been folded in a manner which was not my habit; my watch was unwound. As I regarded this room that I once despised, it appeared to me now a haven and a robust shelter. For those terrible creatures I saw in that evil room, who I only now realize were waiting to suck my blood, would not be able to get in here.

18 May.—I wanted to visit that room again to learn the truth; but when I reached the door I found it locked from the inside. Not only was it locked, but it had been pulled into the frame with such strength that part of the woodwork was splintered. This means that what I saw was not a dream; it was real...

19 May.—No doubt I am in a terrifying situation. Last night the Count told me to write three letters, since my work here was almost done; in the first letter I was to write that my job here was finished and that I would be leaving the castle in a few days; the second letter would say that I was leaving the next day; and the third would make it appear that I had arrived at the hotel in Bistriç. I wanted to object; but in my helpless position, quarreling openly with the Count would be insanity. I was afraid of exciting his anger and suspicion. He explained that the postal service in Transylvania was irregular and that I would ease the minds of my friends in Istanbul if I wrote to them in advance. Despairingly, I gave in and asked him what dates I should put on the letters. After some thought, he said:

"The first letter will be June 12, the second will be June 19, and the third will be June 29!"

Oh! Now I know how long I shall live. God, my great God!

28 May.—Since the last time I wrote in this journal I have imagined a thousand ways to escape and a thousand kinds of torment. I wrote letters to inform those in Istanbul of my situation, but after I awoke one morning I discovered that all of my travel clothes, the writing paper in my bag, and the letters had disappeared. Fortunately I have been carrying this notebook near my breast. In spite of all this, the Count never changes his manner toward me; all we lack are those long, friendly talks. In the morning the Count is nowhere to be seen, as always. At night we only meet at dinner time. As I looked through the window of my room today I saw some Slovakian villagers carrying heavy, rectangular crates to their carriages. I wanted to shout, to give them a sign, but it is impossible. They are too far away. My God, I am going insane. What shall I do, what shall I do?

24 June, before sunrise.—I am still here… I am still in this wretched hell. Last night the Count stayed with me for a while, then went up to his room and locked the door from the inside. A few moments later I rose slowly from the table and went to the window near the spiral staircase to watch for the Count. I saw some gypsies coming and going from the castle, doing something with shovels and pickaxes, and I wanted to discover what was going on.

As I looked out of the window I saw the Count emerge from his, and I hid myself. Bizarrely, the Count was wearing my travel clothes, taken from my room! Then a cold shudder ran through my body. The bag that I saw that night, containing the small child whom those three women passionately and joyfully snatched and ran away with, was hanging around the Count's neck!

Count Dracula again slid down the wall like a lizard and vanished. I decided to wait for his return and made myself comfortable; I began to watch the scenery outside, shimmering in the moonlight. But suddenly I felt a kind of awakening, and it was as if the scenery in front of me began to change. Glittering, quivering dust particles floated in the air and started to whirl round and gather in clusters outside the windows. These bright eddies took weird forms and shapes. Suddenly I understood that I was being hypnotized; with an almost superhuman effort I rose with my eyes wide open and ran to my room, uttering an indescribable scream. For I had seen those three girls again, forming in those shapes!

I waited in my candle-lit room for about two hours with unspeakable feelings. Sometime later a noise issued from the Count's room and suddenly I heard something that sounded like a muted, sharp cry. Then fell a deep, horrible silence. I wanted to run to the door and fling it open, but it was locked. I was trapped here. Exhausted, I sat down on the floor and cried like a baby.

As I sat there with tears in my eyes, I heard the shriek of a woman who sounded as though she were being tortured, and I ran to the window. Yes, there was a woman in the courtyard with dishevelled hair. She was holding her chest as though she had run out of breath from running. When she saw my face in the window, she leapt forward and screamed in a menacing and spiteful voice:

"Monster, give me back my child!"

Then she fell to her knees, raised her hands, and begged and cried. Hearing her, my heart shattered to pieces.

Suddenly, from somewhere high in the castle, I heard the

familiar whisper of the Count. He spoke words that did not sound human, and he was answered from far and wide by the howling of wolves. A few minutes later, packs of wolves filled the courtyard. The poor woman could not even make a sound. I had gone completely mad. I only saw the wolves licking their lips and leaving the courtyard.

But I could not pity the woman. For I knew now what had become of her child, and I said: "It is fortunate its mother died as well!"

What am I going to do? How can I escape this hell, oh dear God!

25 June, morning.—The things that have happened to me repeat every night. I have not once seen the Count in daylight since I have been in this castle. Does this man sleep when everyone is awake and only roam about when all are asleep? Ah, if I could only get into his room just once. But his door is always locked.

And then suddenly it occurred to me: could I not enter his room from the window as he has done? Yes, it is very dangerous, but there is no other choice; what is the worst that could happen? I might fall and die... But would not this death be a hundred times better than that which I endure now—and the hell that awaits me? Perhaps today my interest in sports and gymnastics will profit me. The power, protection, and presence of God grow in my heart.

I entrust you to God, my dear Güzin; farewell dear Rıfat Bey, whom I love as much as my own father! If I die and am lost, will you remember me?

Same day, around noon.—Finally I have made the effort and by the grace of God I have returned to my room alive. I must put down everything as it happened. While I still felt the vigor and courage provoked by the sadness in my heart, I quickly ran to the window above the staircase. Filled with a strength that a man can feel only once or twice in his life, I began to climb the outer wall of the castle like a ladder. My nerves were so tense that I was not frightened by the abyss below. I knew the window the Count had gone in, for I had observed it many times; but when I finally entered it, I felt an intense excitement.

The room was completely empty! The few items that were there were covered in a hundred year-old layer of dust. I searched for the key, but it was nowhere to be seen. However, there was a heap of gold and money stacked in one corner. In this were old gold coins from every nation. Gold coins from Rome, Hungary, Austria, Britain, France, Greece, and Turkey from centuries ago! This pile too had a thick film of dust on top. There was not a single coin in it less than a hundred years old.

When I could not find the keys for the main room and outer doors, I forced another door on the side; I was able to open this one easily. It led to a stone hallway terminating in a steep staircase. I plucked up my courage and descended these dark stairs. A moment later I found myself inside a small, ruined chapel that smelled of mold and freshly dug soil. It seemed to serve as some kind of mausoleum or family grave. There was nothing around of interest to me; but because I saw an open trap door with wide steps a little further on, I decided to go down. This place was some kind of tomb or crypt. There was light coming through from some unknown source, aiding me to see some of the broken tombs and coffins. When my eyes adjusted to this place I noticed that the earth here was freshly dug. There were many large wooden crates in the center of the room.

There, in one of the great boxes of which I counted fifty, all there for some unknown purpose, on a pile of newly dug earth lay the Count! It was impossible to tell if the man was actually dead or just asleep. His eyes were open and as cold and motionless as stone, and he had the frozen look of death on his face. But despite the pallor of body and face, his cheeks showed the vigor and warmth of life and his lips had the same bright red glow. On the other hand, there was no movement in his pulse or heart. By the side of the box was its cover, pierced here and there with holes.

I leaned over the body to search for the door keys. But I saw such a hateful and hostile look in those still, powerless, dead eyes—though surely unconscious of my presence—that I lost all my courage and fortitude. I turned and fled like a lunatic to take shelter in my room.

29 June.—Today is the date of the last of the three letters that the Count made me write. The Count awakened me from sleep, and with surprising kindness he said:

"My friend Azmi Bey, tomorrow you will be leaving. Since I have many things to take care of, we may not be able to see each other again. Tomorrow, some Slovakian villagers and gypsies will come to the castle and move your things. After they leave, my carriage will come and carry you to the mail coach at the Burgo Pass."

He shook my hand firmly. I wanted to say something, to beg him; but he closed the door without looking back. I ran to the door at the last moment. I wanted to force it, to take it apart. But at that moment I heard a whisper from the other side. I stopped and listened, as though hypnotized. The voice of the Count was speaking slowly:

"Back; go back to your place. The time has not yet come. Be patient and wait; you will get what you desire tomorrow night!"

These words were answered by the sensuous, sultry laughter of women. Then, all the voices disappeared.

I walked to the middle of the room and fell down on my knees.

So my end—that terrible, hellish moment—is so near! Tomorrow, tomorrow? Oh great merciful God, help me!

My hands went to my throat. I took my mother's Enâm from its case and began crying and kissing it without even a thought of reading it!

30 June.—The crow of a rooster revealed to me that I had escaped danger for a night. The daylight boosted the confidence and determination that I had lost to fear. I am prepared to do anything to avoid the death that waits for me, grinning with its skeletal face, twelve hours from now. I opened my door and went out. I was determined at any cost to go to the place where I had seen the Count sleeping and take the keys, even if I had to do battle with ghouls. A few moments later I had reached the crypt by way of the window and the gold room. The crate in which the Count slept lay in the same spot; but its lid was also in place, ready to be nailed down.

I opened the lid and set it against the wall. There again lay the Count, but what I saw left me horrified with bewilderment. The Count had become younger, half his age. His white mustache and hair were blackened, leaving only a quarter of his hair white. His cheeks were livelier, his skin had color, and his lips were even redder. And those lips had fresh blood on them. The blood dripped down from the corners of his mouth to his chin and neck! This terrible, ominous creature now looked like a bag filled with blood. I felt an intense disgust as I leaned over the body to touch this corpse. All of my feelings, my soul, rebelled against it. However, I had to search the Count, come what may; it was my last hope. I searched Dracula thoroughly; there was no sign of the keys. Finally, as I ceased my search and looked at the Count's face, I glimpsed such a sinister and mocking smile that it nearly made me go mad. Now I understood many truths. Many trivial, seemingly unrelated events and indications suddenly flashed before my eyes and formed into a clear picture. I was aiding this unthinkably horrible monster to come to Istanbul and my beloved country! There this devil would drink Turkish blood and create a land of devastation like the cursed Impaler Voivode who lived centuries ago. My maddening anger grew even stronger; I thought of saving the world from this evil offspring of the Impaler Voivode. But I had no weapons to cut or dismember him; I saw only a shovel used by the villagers to support the crates. I took it, raised it over my head, and struck, edge downward, that grim, ominous face with all of my strength. As I was delivering my blow, the face of the Count turned halfway toward me and his gaze, full of hatred and evil, fell full upon me. The look nearly paralyzed my hands. My fingers lost their strength and the sharp edge of the shovel turned away from the Count's face. Thus his face was not crushed, but there was a deep gash on his forehead. The shovel fell from my hands to the ground. Pulling the handle away caused the lid to fall into place and hide that horrible sight.

For a moment I thought about what I should do. It was as if my whole brain was on fire. Meanwhile I heard singing and footsteps from far away. That meant the workers and gypsies of whom the Count had spoken were coming. I considered fleeing castle through the door they would enter and running away toward the mountains. I began to run with all my strength to get upstairs as quickly as possible. I went upstairs, entered through the window, and tried to take a quick glance around my room before jumping outside. Alas, the window of the room slammed to with a shock as if a storm had blown it shut. I tried forcing it with all of my strength but it was impossible to open. Once again I was a prisoner in my own room.

As I wrote these lines I could hear some of the carriages moving. Five minutes later, deadly silence had fallen again. There is no question… Right now I am alone in this castle of death with those three terrifying women.

Oh, but I shall not stay here. I will climb down the cliff side of the castle. I will get some gold to take with me just in case. Falling from the cliff and being torn to pieces would be a thousand times better than staying with these monsters. I trust to the grace of the great God. Güzin, my precious Güzin, farewell… I am walking toward death…

CHAPTER V

Letter from Güzin to Şadan.

> *"9 May. Cağaloğlu.*

"Dear Şadan…

"I am very late in answering your letter; please forgive this negligence. If only you knew how much I want to be with you and spend time with you by the sea. I have been very busy lately; a teacher's assistant never has free time. But I also create work for myself. Azmi is now an assistant attorney who can transact business on his own, and I am busy with courses to be able to help him. I have been practicing stenography, learning the typewriter, and whatnot! I will tell you all my plans when we are back together. Of course my fiancé Azmi is also acquainted with them. I just received a short, hastily-written letter from him; he is in Transylvania on important business. Who knows what kinds of things he is seeing in that historic country of the cruel, barbaric Dracula, the Impaler Voivode we read about in our history? You know how much I like those sorts of trips. Oh, the clock is striking ten now. Farewell.

> "Love,
> "GÜZİN

"P.S.—I await all of your news in your letter. You have not written to me for a long time, you naughty thing. Especially about that tall, handsome, curly-haired man!!"

Letter from Şadan to Güzin.

"*Wednesday, Bakırköy.*

"Dearest Güzin;

"How could you send me such a short letter? Is this the answer to all of mine? In any event, I am thankful for what I have. What would I have done if you were completely silent? About that 'tall, handsome, curly-haired' man, I think someone has been spreading rumors and trying to sow discord between us. In any event, do not stay in suspense; the name of this young and handsome man is Turan Bey. He is a major. His parents were friends with my mother and father. He fought in the War of Independence. He is in Istanbul on leave for a couple of months for health reasons. He has an old father and a charming mother. They visit us frequently. He tells us horrible war stories. But he never talks about himself; he is gallant and handsome, but very shy. However, through the major I have made another friend; Doctor Afif Bey. He is young, very kind, and trustworthy. Ah, if you were not engaged to Azmi Bey he would be just the right husband for you. Have I made a faux pas? Please do not be offended. I am sorry; you have your dearest Azmi and he can have you. But there is no harm in my speaking of this doctor! This earnest man was educated in Europe and endured the War of Independence; he tended to our wounded soldiers with the compassion of a father under those poor, horrific conditions. But why do I hesitate? I will tell you all of my secrets here, darling Güzin. That tall, handsome, heroic, and shy staff major Turan Bey and I are in love. And we have confessed it to each other.

"So why should you not know it too? Have we not kept each other's secrets since we were children? God bless you. Güzin, write your reply quickly; start writing as soon as you read this! Write all of your thoughts about me and my news.

That's enough, Güzin. Do not forget me, and pray for my happiness.

"Love,
"ŞADAN"

From Şadan to Güzin.

"*24 May.*

"Dear Güzin,

"Thanks for your sweet reply! Güzin, I have much to tell you in this letter. My Güzin, today I am exactly twenty years old; until today I have never had a marriage proposal. However, I have just had three in the same day. You can imagine how I feel. Three proposals in one day. Isn't it frightening? Believe me when I say I feel a deep pain in my heart for two of the people who proposed to me. On the other hand, I am so happy; I don't know what to do. Let me tell you what happened: but you can never tell anyone! Except Azmi Bey, for if I were you I would tell Azmi Bey all my secrets! But to my story. The first one came before dinner. This was Doctor Afif Bey, who I mentioned to you in my earlier letter! This somber man was very cool outwardly. But when we were alone, I felt something was about to happen between us. When I was alone near the piano, the doctor confessed his love in a very modest, but kind and extremely sincere way, and proposed to me. I was in a very pleasant but troubling position. It was so difficult to turn down this handsome, kind young man and his earnest proposal. But my heart was already connected by an unbreakable bond to someone else. With conflicted feelings, I began to cry. He quickly stood up in a sad and embarrassed manner, apologized for causing me pain, and asked if he might have hope for the future. Then I felt it my duty to tell this young man that the love and dreams of another man were in my heart, and that is what I did. Afif Bey looked pale and his lips quivered. He wanted to say something, but held himself back. Then, with great sincerity, he held my hands, wished me a happy life in the future, and insisted that I consider him a close, dear friend.

"Late afternoon.

"My tall, handsome, curly-haired staff major Turan has just left… I feel bored, and so shall continue to write what occurred.

"Number two came after dinner. This one is also a handsome, scholarly fellow, and what they call an 'original character.' A beautiful specimen of Anatolian man. Raised in the 'Efe' culture of Aydın,[5] he is a tall, heroic-looking, naïve, brave young man. This fellow from Aydın has a lovely name: 'Özdemir Oğuz.' Is that not a name that someone like you, with the heart of a poet, would love? He is also the type that could arouse such feelings. Our Turan Bey, Doctor Afif Bey, and this Özdemir Oğuz all worked together on the front lines of the War of Independence. Turan Bey speaks constantly of what Özdemir Oğuz Bey did at the Uşak front and in rear support.

"This young man from Aydın has also had a good education. His wealthy father sent him to Germany during the Great War; so in short, aside from his sunburnt face and very sweet Aydın accent, he in no way resembles the highlanders. And there is also his sincere manner and almost feminine innocence and purity. Sometimes I think that today's high society Istanbul girls are more unreserved than these young men who were raised by the War of Independence. To make a long story short, this fellow from Aydın, this 'National Forces' squad leader, this young Anatolian man with a good education in Germany, proposed to me in his own way, and it was practically a recurrence of the events between Doctor Afif and myself. But to tell the truth, I think I cried even more this time. Özdemir Oğuz also took my hands in his strong, tanned hands and held them. He even kissed them and said:

---

5   The Efe were the leaders of bands of outlaws and guerilla soldiers in the southwestern Aegean Region of the Ottoman Empire from the 16th to the early 20th centuries. Known for their bravery, they were often perceived by the public as swashbuckling heroes. During the Greco-Turkish War (1919-1922), the Efe joined forces with Mustafa Kemal Atatürk, and during the Turkish War of Independence (1919-1923) they officially joined the ranks of the Turkish national army.

" 'Şadan, you are a warm-hearted and honest girl. If your heart belongs to the man whom I have guessed, and if he knows your value, then I congratulate you both with all my heart, even though I am a little sad. Now I have kissed your hands… This is an agreement of friendship between us. Whatever you need and whenever you wish, you can count on the sacrifice of this young Turk!'

"Güzin, do I need to speak of number three? I don't, do I? Then there is no reason to write the conclusion of the scene between Turan and me. Oh, if I hadn't had to break the hearts of those two precious, honest young men, how happy I would have been! These three men are close friends. Do they talk about me?

"Güzin, it has been a long time. I wait for you with all of my heart. Come, come, come!

"Love and loved by you,
"ŞADAN"

From Güzin's Diary.

24 July. Bakırköy.—I have finally come here, to Şadan. At the station I hugged and kissed her affectionately. Oh, how beautiful this calm, seaside corner of Istanbul is after months of lonely work. We walk around everywhere, Şadan and I; in the mornings and at night we sit and chat on a high hillside overlooking the sea.

But I have one worry; I have not received any letters from Azmi. I wonder why?

26 July. Bakırköy.—I have two pains in my heart: one is not hearing from Azmi, and the other is the condition of Şadan. I asked our dear elder Rıfat Bey, the manager of the business administration office, if he has heard from Azmi by phone. He has received a new, albeit brief letter. Azmi, in his short message, announced that he was preparing to leave Castle Dracula in Transylvania immediately. Oh, the name of that ominous Dracula strains my nerves; I imagine Azmi taken prisoner by the terrible Impaler Voivode. Have I become hysterical?

Rıfat Bey will send me Azmi's letter. I wonder why Azmi has not written to me? Furthermore, there is the concern about Şadan. Lately my childhood friend has had a long-forgotten illness recur. She walks in her sleep. Şadan's mother has spoken to me about it. She warned me to lock the door of our bedroom from the inside and take the keys. Şadan's mother, this sick woman who is already aggrieved; her beautiful daughter is soon to be married. What if word of her problem is made known? According to that poor woman, Şadan's father also had this habit—or to be precise, this illness. It is too bad that this arose just as Şadan and Turan Bey became engaged!

27 July.—There is still no news of Azmi. I have a strange, awful feeling in my heart. Is he ill? Oh, that evil Castle Dracula… What a strange and ugly name; what a coincidence! Şadan still walks in her sleep. I lock the door every night and take the keys. Her poor mother! She cannot tell her daughter about her condition. Nor can I. We have both cried in secret.

3 August.—Another week has passed. There is still no news from Azmi. Not even Rıfat Bey has heard anything. Şadan still gets up in her sleep from time to time and tries to get out. When she finds the door locked she even goes about the room searching for the keys. Poor girl… This breaks my heart so.

6 August.—Three more days and Azmi is still silent. If only I knew his address and could write my reproach to him. I still lament. What if he is ill? Oh God… Şadan is still the same. This is another catastrophe. Her fiancé is coming to stay as a guest. What if Turan Bey learns of her situation and breaks off the engagement? Poor, poor Şadan! I feel a strange sadness when I see her cheerful and healthy countenance in the morning, unaware of the seriousness of her condition!

8 August.—Last night Şadan was very ill. She got up from

her bed twice and left. I caught her in time on both occasions and put her back into bed. My God, what a terrible tragedy; it makes me forget my troubles and Azmi. How hard it is seeing my beautiful, cheerful angel Şadan like this. There was a great storm last night; perhaps it affected her mood.

In the morning Şadan and I went to the same hill we visit every day to watch the sea. There was a large sailing ship right at our feet. Its flag and shape were foreign. We were curious and approached nearer, to the point where the water reached our feet. Large, rectangular crates were being unloaded to land from the ship. We tried to discover what it was to gratify our curiosity. The ship was a Russian one; its flag belonged to the new Bolshevik Soviet government, and these crates were loaded in Varna and contain some kind of clay or sand used for making ceramics. Şadan is so happy when she runs on the sand, and I think about her unnatural behavior at night. It feels like needles have been stuck into my heart. Who would not fall in love with such a beautiful girl? Turan Bey is very lucky. But if only she was not in this accursed situation! Something odd! Sailors are speaking of strange things concerning that ship from Varna; its two passengers and two of its crew disappeared mysteriously and the ship barely made it to the Straits with its three remaining crew members.

11 August, three o'clock.—I write these lines with great agitation. I have gone through horrible things and an agonizing experience. After writing in my journal last night I went to sleep. I do not know for how long, but I woke up with an unpleasant pain and felt cold. The room was dark. I could not see Şadan's bed. I leapt from mine and felt hers; the bed was empty. I found a match on the table and lit it, and suddenly I noticed that the key had been taken from the table drawer and the door was unlocked. That meant that Şadan had woken up again and gone outside. I turned on the light and checked the sofa and the parlor, but there was no one there. As an ever-growing fear chilled my heart, I continued to check all the other rooms. Şadan Hanım wasn't there. I went downstairs, and the front door to the garden was wide open. Because we kept this door carefully closed, I began to fear that Şadan had gone out to the garden or the street in her nightdress. At that moment there was no worry in my mind except Şadan. With courage that I was surprised I possessed, I put on something and quickly went outside. There was no one in the garden; the full moon had turned the night into day, so I had no difficulty seeing the whole scene, even far away. I moved from the garden to the square. There was no one around, but the fact that the garden gate was open told me that Şadan was out there. Suddenly I thought of the hillside overlooking the sea where we would go each day and sit for hours. Had she gone there in her unconscious, sleepwalking state out of habit? I began to run in that direction and soon discovered that my guess had not been wrong. Far away at our beautiful conversation spot, on that large rock, she was leaning forward under the faint rays of the moonlight, white as a ghost. Just at that moment, a black cloud covered the face of the moon; but before it went dark I noticed another long, black shape standing behind that white figure. What was it? I could not tell if it was man or beast. I did not stop to think it over, but ran in that direction. The path leading to the hillside fell and rose quickly at one point. When I ascended after passing that low point, I saw Şadan again on the hillside in front of me. Yes, there was a black shape next to her. This black thing leaned over the white figure which lay half-reclining. I called to Şadan in fright and agitation. The bright face of the moon was again hidden behind clouds. I ran even faster. When I finally reached the rock on the hillside I found Şadan alone; there was no sign of any living creature around. Şadan was almost frozen, her neck angled to one side. She was gasping for air as though she had stopped breathing for some time. When I came near her, she put her hand to the collar of her nightdress and pulled it back around her throat. I saw she was shaking from head to toe; I quickly took the heavy shawl from my shoulders and covered her. I fastened the shawl around her throat with a pin I found, but I may have let the pin touch her skin; for once she started breathing normally again, I saw her touch her throat and moan in pain. I could not afford to waste any more time. Shaking her slightly, I woke her up and told her to take my arm and come home quickly. I was afraid that she might be surprised, but she rose immediately and began walking like an obedient child. I took off my slippers and put them on her feet. To avoid them being seen by anyone, I put my feet into a little puddle of mud on the way back home. We were lucky, for we arrived home without being seen by a soul. Şadan was shaking and my heart was racing. We washed our feet and I put my poor friend into her bed. Before going to sleep, Şadan asked me not to tell anyone about this sleepwalking incident, even her mother. Although I hesitated at first to grant her request, thinking of how sorry her mother would be if she were to hear, and how other people would exaggerate this incident, I promised her that I would keep quiet.

As I write these lines, Şadan is sound asleep and the morning sun is shining over the Marmara waters.

12 August.—I awoke twice tonight and saw Şadan trying to open the door. Even in this state, she appeared almost angry at being unable to find the keys. I took her arm and put her into bed, despite her resistance. Oh my great God, how I wonder about Azmi. I do not want to say it, but something, some disaster has occurred.

13 August.—Tonight I slept with the key tied to my waist again. I do not know what awoke me. Şadan was sitting up in bed, still asleep, pointing at the window with indescribable fear. I got up softly and looked outside. Moonlight shone everywhere. The light danced over the broad surface of the Marmara Sea; between the moon and the window a huge bat circled in the air. However, at some point it must have seen me because it went away immediately. It flew off toward the village graveyard. When I came away from the window, Şadan was sleeping in great peace and comfort.

14 August.—Şadan is practically in love with the rock on the hill where we watch the sea. She goes there to sit and think deeply. Late this afternoon we were sitting in that very place. She was lost in thought. Looking off at some unknown point, she murmured:

"Those red eyes again! They are just the same…"

I leaned down quickly. I followed her eyes. Far away from us there sat a strange, solitary man in black clothes. For a moment this man's eyes appeared blazing red! Yet when I looked more closely, the illusion was dispelled. It had to have been a trick of the last light of sunset. Şadan rose from her place with a somber expression. We came home without saying a word. Şadan had a headache and went to sleep early. I went out through the front garden; after lying by the sea and thinking about Azmi with deep sorrow, I returned. It was bright as day again. As I came home, I looked up at the windows of the house; ours was open. I saw that Şadan was leaning out of the window and looking around. I waved my handkerchief, thinking she was looking out for me, but she did not react. When I was under the window, I saw Şadan had fallen asleep with her head on the windowsill. A rather large bird was standing in front of her. Thinking that she would get a chill, I ran quickly inside the house. When I came into the room Şadan was up and returning to her bed, again asleep and breathing very heavily. She put her hand to her throat as though she were trying to shield herself from the cold. I put her gently onto her bed without waking her. Then I shut the door and window firmly. At that moment I noticed something. Şadan's face was deathly pale. Black circles had formed under her eyes. She sleeps so poorly; I almost feel afraid for her.

15 August.—Today I woke late, but Şadan slept even longer than me. We had some very good news. Turan Bey's father, who was very sick in Erenköy, has been getting better. For that reason the wedding between Turan Bey and Şadan will be hastened. Şadan's mother is both glad and grieved. I spoke to her in private for a moment. This strong, warm-hearted woman told me that she was informed by her doctor that her disease is very serious, and that there is almost no possibility of surviving her heart condition. We will never let Şadan know. According to the doctor, because this woman's heart is weakening every day, a tragic end may come in three or four months. I was wise not to tell this poor woman that Şadan went out into the street in her sleep, for she might have died on the spot.

17 August.—I have not picked up my journal for two days. I am frightened. I feel that there is a shadow of misfortune and sorrow over us. There is still no news from Azmi. Şadan keeps getting weaker, paler, and sicker. I cannot understand for the life of me why this poor girl is withering away like this. She eats well and enjoys the fresh air. I lock the door every night and hide the key against my chest. She wakes up and usually sits in front of the open window. Last night I found her looking as though she were about to faint. I was hardly able to wake her. She does not remember how she opened the window. She sobbed silently on my shoulder. I wonder if the pinprick from when we were sitting on the hill, when I tried to put the shawl around her neck, has caused this illness. I looked at her neck while she was asleep tonight. That small wound has not closed and, in fact, it has become larger. And the edges of the wound are a little white… If it does not close in a day or two I will certainly take her to a doctor.

18 August.—I have a part of my sanity back. There is still no news from Azmi, but at least Şadan is feeling a little better. She is happy again. Today we were sitting in our old place and joking around. Taking advantage of this, I asked if she had dreamed on that night she came here. All of a sudden she became serious; there was even a hint of sadness on her face. She said, softly:

"I didn't quite dream; in fact, I was almost awake. I felt a very strong urge to come here. However, I was also afraid of something. Yes, I was asleep. But I faintly remember going out into the street and coming here. At one point I saw a dark shape and, just as we saw the other night, it had red eyes. I felt as though I was drowning in deep, green water. There were sweet voices in my ears. I felt like my blood was drained from my body and I lost myself in a bittersweet pleasure. Then I remember you waking me up."

She suddenly began to laugh. It seemed a little uncanny and wild to me. When we came home, Şadan's cheeks were very rosy and her unnatural cheerfulness was still there.

19 August.—Ah, how happy I am, my God, I finally received news from my dear Azmi. My Azmi has been sick; that is why he has not written to me. He is now staying at Edirne Hospital. I am leaving by train tomorrow. I saw Rıfat Bey; he was both delighted and sad. Laughing, he told me, "When you go to Edirne, please marry Azmi immediately." What a kind and thoughtful man; only a father could be so compassionate. Worrying about him and missing him will keep me awake tonight. There is a very strange explanation in the letter that the hospital's manager sent to Rıfat Bey. Hungarian police found Azmi in a city in a very miserable way, looking almost like a madman, and from the documents on him it was understood that he was Turkish. He was turned over to our consulate and sent back to Edirne. He has had a nervous breakdown. And now he is quite exhausted.

Letter from Major Turan Bey to Doctor Afif Bey.

"31 August.

"Dear Afif,

"I have a great favor to ask of you. Şadan is very sick; she is almost wasting away. When I finally arrived from Erenköy to visit her, I was surprised and troubled. My dear friend, or rather my dear brother, I trust in your skill and candor. I have just been called back to Erenköy due to my father's illness; I must leave. You must check up on Şadan without alerting her mother. The rest is up to you. Send me a telegram in Erenköy if necessary.

"With all my love,
"Your brother: TURAN"

Letter from Doctor Afif Bey to Turan.

"I have carried out your request. First let me hasten to say that, thanks to God, after my examination I found no sign of illness in Şadan Hanım. However, I did not like her condition at all. She is woefully different from the last time I saw her. I have not found a chance to examine or speak to her closely. To outside appearances, I found Şadan Hanım cheerful while her mother was with us. After dinner, her mother left and I was alone with Şadan Hanım. Once all were gone, her gaiety deserted her. She lowered her head in great exhaustion and covered her face with her hands. I took advantage the situation and asked her what was wrong, explaining that I was here at your request. She said, 'I don't want to talk about myself; I only think and worry about Turan!'

"I took some of her blood that day and tested it; there is nothing abnormal about it. In fact, it shows in itself a vigorous state of health. However, there is no doubt that Şadan Hanım has some kind of ailment. In my opinion it is something mental. She complains about occasional shortness of breath, fainting, and heavy sleep. She has nightmares from time to time as well. She also said this: she had a sleepwalking illness when she was a child. Recently she has begun to relapse. One night she walked out of the house and went as far as a hill by the sea; her friend Güzin Hanım found her there. But she assures me that in the last few days the habit has not returned. I have concerns about this situation and have done something that I felt would be appropriate. I would have done the same were it my dear sister. I do not know what you will think of it. I wrote a letter to my old tutor, my most dear and trusted friend Resuhî Bey, who is now living a secluded life in Yakacık, and asked him to come immediately. You know Resuhî Bey, for I often used to tell his strange stories in Anatolia. The whole country knows his reputation. Even my French colleagues have told me, on occasion, what a credit he is to our nation. Strangely, his work is more well-known to Westerners than to Turks. We call him 'Mad Resuhî' and move on. If only Turkey had half a dozen more mad men like him. Resuhî Bey is indeed a great expert in mental illnesses. I am quite sure that he will succeed where I fail.

"Your brother: Dr. Afif"

From Doctor Resuhî Bey to Doctor Afif Bey.

"2 September.

"My dear friend,

"It is such a strange coincidence; I was about to visit you in Istanbul when I received your letter. I have not yet come down to Istanbul this summer. I have very much wished to see you. Even were this not so, I should have rushed to Istanbul after your letter. Tell this truth to your friend whose fiancée is ill: There is no possible way for Doctor Resuhî to refuse any request from the Doctor Afif who courageously sucked the gangrene poison from the wound on my arm caused by a knife thrown by his friend in a moment of anger in the middle of a very important operation.

"In any event, I am coming soon… Wait for me!

"Resuhî"

From Doctor Afif to Turan Bey.

"Dear friend,

"Doctor Resuhî Bey has come and gone back to Yakacık. Of course he examined Şadan Hanım discretely without alerting her sick mother. He examined her carefully and is to report to me, and I shall advise you. My old friend appears to be taking this matter seriously, but he says he must think it through first. My tutor has strange habits. He is the most radical scientist of the modern age, but he also has odd beliefs. That is why he is a target for so many envious people. When the old man says, 'Let me think,' it is impossible to get any more out of him. But his final word is always plain. That is why

I ask you not to be angry with my tutor. You can trust him implicitly. I think the fact that he is placing so much importance on this is better for us. After a long examination of Şadan Hanım, he said these very words to me: 'You are right, there is no physical illness visible on this little miss. But I see she has lost much blood. Strangely, I cannot understand why. But I will; I will think about it. I must return to my home in Yakacık today. You must send me a telegram every day; I can be here in two hours if need be. This charming, angelic creature interests me too.' As he spoke this, the thick, black eyebrows of my old professor were knit and his face showed immense gravity. There, my brother Turan, now you know as much about Şadan's illness as I do. I will focus absolutely all of my care and attention on observing her. I am already near her home. I hope your father is well. I imagine that his condition, while Şadan Hanım is in such a state, is a heavy weight on your mind. If this had not happened, you would be together with Şadan Hanım and that would have a great effect on her. I will let you know every little detail, my brother, do not worry."

Telegram from Doctor Afif to Doctor Resuhî Bey.

"6 September.
"Şadan Hanım has had terrible change after being well and happy for two days. I will not inform her fiancé before your visit."

CHAPTER VI

FROM DOCTOR AFİF BEY'S DIARY

When Doctor Resuhî Bey came from Yakacık to see me, his first words were, "Have you notified Şadan's fiancé Turan Bey about her condition?"

"No!" I said. The Doctor seemed pleased. "That is very good. Very good indeed! Better not to know anything for now. I hope to God that he will never have to know. However, if he must, he will learn everything. Now Afif, let me tell you something: the two of us, and only us, will know the things that we shall learn while working together. I have some thoughts and plans. You will understand them when the time comes, but until that time hold your tongue and open your eyes. Notify me of every significant change."

When I described Şadan's recent symptoms, his old solemnity grew even greater, but he did not say one word. When we saw Şadan, I became even more concerned than I had been before. The poor child was as white as a corpse, chalkily pale. The redness had gone from her lips and even her gums. The bones of her face were prominent. Her faint breathing would have been painful for anyone to see. My old tutor was as still as a statue, his bushy eyebrows almost converging above his nose. Şadan lay on her bed and looked as though she could not find the strength to say a word. A deep and heavy silence hung over us. Presently my tutor gave me a meaningful glance. I understood, and we both left the room. He took me into the opposite room, looked around, closed the door, and said:

"Oh my God! This is terrible, very terrible! We do not have a moment to lose. Little Şadan will die for sheer want of enough blood for her heart. We must give her a transfusion immediately. According to an earlier blood test of Şadan Hanım, we all have the same blood type. Now tell me, will it be yours or mine?"

"Sir, I am both younger and stronger than you. It is unquestionably my responsibility."

"Then get ready; I will bring my medical bag from downstairs."

I went downstairs with Resuhî Bey when, just at that moment, Turan burst in the room. When he saw me, he grasped my hand.

"Your letter had me worried; my father is doing better now, so I took the chance," he said. Then Turan noticed the professor and greeted him in a sincere but military fashion.

"Doctor Resuhî Bey, I believe. Sir, I have no words to tell you how grateful I am."

When Resuhî Bey saw Şadan's fiancé enter at such an inconvenient time, his eyes flashed suddenly with anger. But Turan Bey's heroic appearance, his handsome face full of life, and his eyes shining with the light of innocence and bravery quickly made this anger disappear and transformed it into a gleam of happiness.

Without ceremony he held out his hand and said:

"You came just in time, Turan Bey. You are the fiancé of Şadan Hanım. She is very, very sick… Nay, my child, do not be so pessimistic! You shall help her now. Be brave!"

Turan, whose face had turned pale at the doctor's first words, asked:

"Tell me, what can I do? My body and blood belong to Şadan. I would give the last drop of blood in my body for her."

The old doctor could be humorous in even the gravest situations;

"No, no… I don't ask so much of your blood as that." He put his hand on Turan's shoulder. "You are stronger than Doctor Afif here and myself. My child, let me tell you this, because Şadan is like my daughter! She is very weak. I spoke with Afif before you arrived. We had decided to give her blood to save her from death. From the test we performed we know that both of our blood types are a match for Şadan Hanım, but since Afif is younger and stronger than I am, he was to be the one to give it." At that moment Turan grasped my hand and shook it firmly. "However, there is no need if you are here. Your blood is stronger than Afif's. Come! First we must know your blood type." The old professor quickly tested Turan's blood. By a great coincidence, the blood types of Turan and Şadan were also the same.

Turan stood outside the door. Resuhî Bey and I went into Şadan's room; she turned her head slowly to look at us. But that was all. She looked too weak to say a word. Resuhî Bey gave her a narcotic. The poor child swallowed the drug without resistance, but with great difficulty. Presently she was deeply asleep. The doctor called Turan into the room and asked him to take off his jacket. Then, in a gentle and courteous tone he said:

"You may now take one kiss from your fiancée." And he turned to me quickly and said, walking to the far end of the room:

"Come here Afif, help me get these tools!"

I understood that these last words from the doctor were so that Turan could take a kiss from this sleeping angel.

Doctor Resuhî Bey performed the blood transfusion quickly and skillfully. As the young, strong blood began to course through her veins, Şadan's face began to change color and appear almost rosy. On the other hand, my brave friend Turan, who had not blanched even as he marched toward enemy lines, was turning pale as his blood continued to be withdrawn; yet his eyes shone with joy and pride. Although I felt angry as I saw what the loss of blood had turned this young man into, I could not understand how this young woman had lost so much blood in so short a time. Meanwhile the professor had his watch in his hand. When the blood transfusion was completed, Resuhî Bey gently adjusted the girl's pillow. That caused the locket on her neck to move and expose a small wound. Turan did not notice it, as he was tired, but I heard Doctor Resuhî Bey sigh heavily as he does when he is very troubled. My old tutor said nothing about this, but turned to me and said:

"Now give our hero Turan Bey some champagne, and after he rests here for a while, send him home to have a hearty meal, get a good night's sleep, and warn him not walk around too much. Turan Bey, my friend, we do not need you here any longer. Now you need to rest. When Şadan Hanım wakes up, I shall tell her all about your sacrifice."

Turan Bey could not argue with these authoritative words, so he shook the doctor's hands and went out. After seeing Turan off, I returned to the patient's room. The old doctor was watching her intently, oblivious to his surroundings. The high collar of Şadan's velvet dress again covered her red wound. Suddenly Resuhî Bey turned to me and asked very softly:

"What do you make of this wound on Şadan's neck?"

"I have not seen it very well," I said, and lifted her collar gently to examine it. There were two small punctures just over the vein on her neck. The surrounding area was white and looked as if it had been touched and bruised. At first I thought to myself, *Did this girl lose all her blood from these small wounds?* But that was not possible.

Resuhî Bey locked his eyes on mine and asked:

"Well?"

"To be honest, I can make nothing of it."

At this, he immediately rose and said: "I must go to Yakacık tonight! There are books and other things which I need; you will stay here and keep your eyes on Şadan!"

"Shall I call a nurse?"

"Are there any better nurses than us? You will keep watch

all night; see that she is well fed and that nothing disturbs her. As I have said, you must not sleep at all tonight. Later we will have our time to sleep. I shall be back as soon as possible."

After saying this he left the room, but came back again a moment later, raised his finger and said:

"Remember, I am leaving Şadan in your charge. If something happens to her, you shall suffer until you die."

Doctor Afif Bey's Diary—continued.

8 September.—I sat up all night with Şadan. The opiate she was given lost its effect around evening. She woke up naturally; she had changed almost completely. She was cheerful and energetic. When I told her mother that Resuhî Bey had tasked me with sitting by her daughter's side all night, the poor woman practically made fun of me, repeating how strong and happy she was. Naturally I avoided telling this sick woman what had occurred earlier. Şadan ate her supper, and I sat in my chair near the bedside. She did not speak, but when my eyes met hers I could sense a deep feeling of gratitude. Some time later she seemed to be sinking off to sleep, but she visibly attempted to resist. This was repeated several times. It was clear that Şadan did not wish to sleep. When I noticed this, I asked:

"You do not want to sleep?"

"No, I am afraid."

"Afraid to go to sleep? I don't understand."

"If you were in my situation, you would have the same fear. Sleep is presage of horror to me!"

"What do you mean?"

"Oh, I don't know, I don't know! That is what frightens me, not knowing… This weakness always comes to me when I sleep."

"But Şadan Hanım, I am here tonight; rest assured that nothing will happen to you. Sleep well!"

This poor girl: "I believe you, I do," she said. Then she took a deep breath and fell asleep. The night passed very calmly. In the morning I left the house and notified both

Turan Bey and Doctor Resuhî Bey by telegram, telling them of the excellent result of the blood transfusion and the night's rest.

9 September.—After work I returned to Şadan Hanım's house. I was very tired, for I had not had any sleep for two nights and two days. Şadan appeared to me cheerful and rested. We ate a family meal heartily. When I took Şadan to her room, she looked at me and said:

"You have changed so much… Tonight, no sitting up with me. I am very well and if you do not sleep, I shall not sleep either. Look, there is a room next to you; you can sleep on this sofa. The door between our rooms can stay open and if I feel worse, I can ring this bell. That way it will be as if we are in the same room."

I could not but acquiesce. I was dead tired and without sleep. I could not have sat up if I had tried. After making Şadan promise that she would wake me up for even the smallest of things, I lay down on the sofa and fell asleep immediately.

I started as a hand touched my head. In the national struggle, those bloody and terrible guerilla days, and later in the regular army, it was a habit for us to bolt from sleep while remaining completely calm and lucid. How many times did I have to take up arms with Turan and Özdemir immediately upon waking. However, this time I was not rising in the Uşak mountains, the Polatlı hills, or the Aydın fog. The strong hands of my dear tutor, Doctor Resuhî Bey, were rousing me in Şadan's house.

The first words from the professor were:

"How is the patient?"

"Well," I said.

"Let us go and see."

We both went into Şadan's room; the curtains were closed and I opened them slowly. As he looked toward the bed, Doctor Resuhî Bey sighed sharply; I knew very well what this meant. I froze with fear. As I attempted to make out the situation, he moved back with cries of "Oh God!" Every muscle of his face expressed great fear and agony. He raised his hands and pointed to the bed. I could feel my knees trembling.

There on the bed lay poor Şadan, unconscious and even more anemic than the other day!

Even her lips were chalky white; her gums seemed to have receded.

The old professor raised his left foot to stamp the ground in anger, but quickly regained control and opened his bag. He moistened Şadan's lips with a medicine and rubbed her wrists and forehead. After listening to her heart with great care and anxiety he said:

"It is not too late. She has a pulse, though it is very weak. All my work is undone. We must start again. Today her fiancé Turan Bey is not here; so Afif, my friend, it is up to you!"

As he spoke, Resuhî produced the necessary equipment from the large bag which had everything he needed. Though I felt my face blush, I took off my jacket without a word. The blood transfusion began; time felt as though it were passing more slowly, for two reasons. On one hand, giving blood was making me drowsy; on the other hand, I was worried that Şadan was showing no improvement. Finally, with a joy and relief I cannot describe, I saw her pale skin become rosier. No man can know until he experiences it what it is to feel his own life-blood running through the veins of the woman he loves!

When the blood transfusion was over and Doctor Resuhî was attending to Şadan, I bandaged my wound; I felt as though I were about to faint. As I went downstairs to have a glass of wine upon the advice of Resuhî Bey, the old professor ran after me and said:

"Remember, you must never mention this operation to anyone. Off you go."

I lay down on my side as I drank the wine, wondering how Şadan could have lost so much blood in one night, and fell asleep. But awake or asleep, the small wounds on Şadan's neck flashed ever before my eyes.

After sleeping all day, Şadan awoke fairly well, though not nearly so much so as the day before. Seeing her condition, Doctor Resuhî went out for a walk. He warned me not to leave the patient alone for even a moment. I heard Resuhî Bey ask the maid about a telegraph office.

Şadan chatted with me freely; it was obvious that she was unaware of this new incident. After two hours, Resuhî Bey returned and said:

"Now go home, eat plenty of nutritious food, and sleep. I am here; do not say anything about the situation here to anyone; I have very important reasons for this. No! Do not ask now, but keep in mind that even impossible things can happen. Good bye!"

11 September.—Once I felt better, I went to see Şadan. I found the doctor in excellent spirits and Şadan as happy and healthy as Resuhî Bey. After my arrival, a large suitcase from Yakacık arrived for the old professor.

The doctor opened the suitcase; he presented a rather large bundle of white flowers to Şadan and said:

"Şadan Hanım, these are for you. But they are not a gift; they are a medicine. Oh little miss, do not frown. Do not be afraid, I shall not boil them and make you drink it. I will put them up like trimming around your windows and make a wreath of them for you to wear around your neck; then you shall be able to sleep soundly."

Şadan had every reason to frown; these were nothing but garlic flowers. When Şadan threw the bundle from her hands in disgust, Resuhî Bey knit his eyebrows.

"Nooo, Şadan Hanım, I do not want such jokes; in everything I do there is a very important and significant purpose," he said. When the doctor saw Şadan was becoming distressed, he softened his voice and held her hand. "My daughter, my child! I am working for your own good. For God's sake, for the love of all the people who love you so much, listen to my words... Look, I will put these flowers around your room with my own hands, and I am making your necklace too. But you must never mention these to anyone. Come, Afif, let us decorate the windows and the room. I had them pick these flowers especially from the villages of Yakacık."

Doctor Resuhî Bey's actions were very strange and mysterious. Even I was troubled by this exercise in the name of medicine. Resuhî Bey first closed the windows tightly and put the shutters in place; then he carefully lined the window frames and windows with the flowers. He did the same to the door. Presently I lost my patience and asked my old tutor:

"Professor, I have never seen you do anything contrary to logic and scientific reason, but if someone saw you here now they would think you were casting a spell on the room to keep out evil spirits."

Resuhî Bey, fastening the wreath in his hands, said calmly:

"Perhaps I am!"

Then he put the wreath around Şadan's neck:

"Do not disturb this; and even if it is very hot tonight, do not open the window or door!"

When we left the room my old friend turned to me and said:

"Tonight I can sleep in peace; and sleep I need. Tomorrow, come to my hotel and we will both go to visit our little miss; you will see that my spell will have healed her!" (At this, the doctor laughed strangely.)

CHAPTER VII

From Şadan Hanım's Diary.

12 September.—I should like to write a few things in my diary while I feel well. Ah, this old doctor Resuhî Bey is a venerable, kind person. I quite love him. What of Doctor Afif? He is really an angel; that is what you call a true friend. I am happy that I am surrounded by such compassionate people as Turan and my mother!

Oh my God, what were all these struggles I have had against sleep, and those terrible dreams? How blessed are some people who can sleep comfortably. Tonight I hope I may join them. I have never loved garlic but tonight it almost smells delightful. Come, sweet slumber. I entrust all to God. Tonight I will not fear the sound of wings flapping outside my window!

From Doctor Azmi Bey's Diary.

13 September.—I called on Doctor Resuhî Bey; we got into an automobile and went to see Şadan Hanım. After passing the sweet smell of the garden on this lovely morning, we met Şadan's mother, always an early riser, downstairs. The woman said with a cheerful expression:

"I congratulate and thank you, doctors; Şadan is very well.

In fact, seeing as she is not yet up, she must be sleeping perfectly. I did not enter her room lest I should disturb her. But doctors, do not claim all the credit for yourselves. I woke up in the night and went into her room to check on her. She was sleeping like an angel, but the room was full of foul-smelling flowers. Şadan even had a wreath of them around her neck. I took them all away so that this foul smell would not bother my daughter, and opened a window to let in some air. Have I not done well, gentlemen?"

Upon saying this, she went away to her room. I looked at the old professor; his face instantly turned white. He remained calm in front of this poor woman who was susceptible to death from the slightest shock. But the moment she left, he grasped my hand in great anger and took me into one of the rooms and closed the door.

Then, for the first time, I saw this calm man break down under the weight of hardship and sorrow! He raised his hands, beat them upon his knees, sat down in a chair, and in a quiet but terrible voice began to sob like a desperate child. This went on for a minute or two. Resuhî Bey raised his hands again and screamed as though appealing to the whole universe.

"My God, my God, my God! What have we done? What has this poor girl done to suffer so much tragedy? Has the pagan world of old sent its evil spirits to us? Are we yet dealing with a talisman of doom?

"This poor woman, in order to make her comfortable, is unknowingly destroying her dear daughter's life, blood, and soul! The worst is, we can tell her nothing…"

Then he leapt up suddenly:

"Come, Afif; we must see and act. Be it demon or magic, we will fight this evil and not lose hope."

He took his bag; we went into Şadan's room. When Doctor Resuhî saw her, he said, "Just as I thought… she is unconscious again!" He locked the door from the inside and began removing his instruments from the bag. There would be a third blood transfusion.

This time we transferred some of my generous and brave

tutor's blood into Şadan's veins. The poor girl began to breathe normally again. Her white lips and cheeks grew redder and she fell into a healthy sleep. Before leaving her to rest, Resuhî Bey saw Şadan's mother and warned her sternly not to touch anything in the patient's room.

I consider myself a good doctor, but I do not understand any of this. Is it because all the worry, fear, and distress is making me dimwitted?

From Şadan's Diary.

17 September.—I have had peace for four days and four nights. I am recovering very quickly, as though I have been spared from a long and dark nightmare. Now I barely remember the hours of waiting and dreading. My God, what was it? I was falling into an oblivion of darkness and amnesia at night, and opening my eyes tired and nearly dead in my bed. After the dear Doctor Resuhî Bey's mental treatments, I am free of all of my troubles. I no longer hear the flapping wings of a big, dark bird at night. I no longer hear distant, strange, and harsh orders telling me to do things against my will. Now I can fall asleep without being afraid. I have grown accustomed to the smell of garlic flowers; Doctor Resuhî Bey brings baskets of them every day. I decorate my room with the flowers and close up everything. I awoke twice last night. Resuhî Bey was asleep on the sofa; and even though I heard the angry sound of wings flapping, I easily fell asleep again.

17 September, night.—I write these lines to leave an exact record of what has happened. Let it be clear that if I die, no one is responsible. Yes… I feel that I am about to die soon of exhaustion. However, I will keep writing with all of my remaining strength. I will even die with the pen in my hand.

After seeing that the flowers had been placed as Doctor Resuhî Bey directed, I went to sleep in peace. I awoke suddenly in the middle of the night. Outside the window I heard the sound of flapping wings that had begun the night my dear friend Güzin found me by the seaside in Bakırköy. I did not have the same fear and strange feeling of helplessness, but I would have liked Resuhî Bey to be here in the next room. I tried to sleep, but it was impossible. Presently the old fear of sleep returned, and I determined to keep awake. As if in spite, drowsiness began to come over me. I got out of bed and looked against my will toward the window. A large bat was visible in the darkness, buffeting its wings against the glass from time to time. I decided to go back to bed, although not to sleep, but just at that moment my mother came into the room and sat on the bed beside me. She kissed my cheeks and said, "I was worried about you, my girl!" I was afraid that she might be cold because of her thin nightdress. So I convinced her to sleep next to me. As we lay there, the flapping of wings came to the window again. My mother was startled a little and asked, "What is that?" I tried to pacify her but I could almost hear the heavy beating of her heart.

A minute later the flapping sound grew louder. With one last blow, the window shattered into the room and a strong wind blew the curtains toward us. My mother pointed at the window and screamed. For there, a red-eyed, gaunt old wolf— yes, a real wolf—was staring at us with bared teeth. My mother uttered a silent groan following her scream and afterward fell still; but at that moment she clutched the wreath of flowers around my neck and broke it apart. I could not think clearly about anything; my eyes were fixed on the broken window. The wolf drew his head back, and the wind filled the room with thousands of glittering specks and spots of dust. These shiny things scattered, swirled, and formed strange shapes. I wanted to move but I was anchored in place as if by some invisible force. The cold body of my mother, who had died because her heart could not withstand the terror, lay on my chest. After this I blacked out completely for some time.

When I opened my eyes, my whole body was shaking and I lay with my mother's dead body. I was barely able to write these lines in the diary beneath my head. There, those bright spots, those tiny specks are beginning to float again... My God, my God, protect me. My brave lover Turan, where are you? Farewell Turan, my eyes are closing, I am getting worse. I do not think I can write any more… my God…

From Doctor Afif's Diary.

18 September.—When I approached the door of Şadan's house this morning, I saw Resuhî Bey stepping out of an automobile. There was a great commotion in the house, and even crying. My old tutor's face was completely white.

We went straight to Şadan's door without a word to anyone. Oh God, how can I describe the scene we saw there!

Two women lay on the bed: Şadan and her mother. The old woman was surely dead. With her deathly pale face, Şadan looked no different. Her throat was bare; those two eerie wounds were visible on her neck, but this time the area around them was badly mangled. Resuhî Bey began carefully listening to her chest. Then he stepped back suddenly and cried out:

"We still have a chance. Quick, quick! Bring me that bottle!"

I leapt up and brought the medicine bottle from the bag left near the door; the doctor moistened Şadan's lips, gums, wrists, and forehead. As we worked, one of the servants entered the room slowly and informed us that a man sent by Turan Bey was waiting. I said simply, "Take him upstairs!" and returned to what I was doing. I have never seen Resuhî Bey work so earnestly. He massaged Şadan very gently, as though he were afraid to break her. At that moment, he turned to me and said these incomprehensible words:

"If it would only end in death, by God's will, I would leave this poor girl to the angel of death. But what might come next is horrible, very horrible."

After continuing his work with great care and vigor he said: "We are winning, we have won the first round; her body temperature is normalizing. But there is a problem: Şadan needs another blood transfusion, and very quickly. If not, the poor girl shall not live an hour. However, we have taken your blood, and I am useless after giving blood the last time. Now, where will we find the brave man who will open his veins and spill his blood for Şadan one more time?"

At that very moment, we heard a powerful voice from the doorway. The words, spoken with an Aydın accent, filled my heart with joy:

"Very well, what's wrong with me?"

We both turned; there, with his tall frame, sunburn, shining black eyes, and handsome face, was my friend from Germany and the War of Independence, Özdemir Bey.

My old tutor started when he heard this loud voice, but when I said, "Ah, Özdemir, is it you?" and reached out to him, Resuhî Bey's frown disappeared. Özdemir Bey took a long, sorrowful look at the bed; his face turned pale, but he held himself with his usual superhuman steadfastness:

"Turan sent me. He said that he has not heard from you for three days; he is worried sick about Şadan Hanım. However, his father is very ill; the old man does not let his son out of his sight for a moment. That is why he had to send me instead."

Doctor Resuhî Bey suddenly strode forward, grasped Özdemir's powerful hands, and looked him straight in the eyes:

"Özdemir Bey, when a woman is in trouble, the most effective medicine is a man's blood! I see you are one of the bravest and most honest men in these Turkish lands. No matter how much the devil fights us, God always sends us men when we want them."

I will not go into detail; we performed the blood transfusion once again. However, this time Şadan had been too depleted; even though Özdemir's veins were pumping out more blood than any of ours had done, the action of her heart and lungs was barely detectable. I took the exhausted Özdemir to another room and set him on the bed to rest, after first giving him something to drink. When I returned to Şadan's room, Doctor Resuhî Bey was holding a little notebook; he had evidently read it for he was deep in thought. He looked up for a moment; he had the harsh, bitter countenance of someone who has just assumed the burden of some cryptic thing. He passed the notebook to me, saying only:

"I found this on Şadan's bed!"

Upon reading the notebook, I turned to him and asked, "For the love of God, tell me, what does all of this mean? Is Şadan mad? What kind of ominous and terrible danger is this?" Resuhî Bey took the diary from me.

"Do not trouble about it now," he said, "you shall understand everything when the time comes."

I could ask no more of my tutor; there was not time enough anyway. I went to the post office immediately, sending a telegram to Turan informing him that Şadan's mother was dead, but that Şadan had regained her health. A few hours later, Özdemir Bey had revived. He sat me down by his side, took my hand, looked at me, and said:

"Afif, Turan Bey told me everything. One by one we all fell in love with Şadan Hanım and wished to marry her; the lottery chose Turan and they both deserve each other, and may God make them happy. However, I am ever prepared to sacrifice my life for Şadan. Our friendship amid hundreds of deaths has placed this duty on your shoulders and mine. But as I understand, the heroic-looking old Doctor upstairs also gave his blood to Şadan Hanım. Please tell me, what has caused this girl to lose so much blood?"

I did not know myself. I could not speak of the strange things I had seen after Resuhî Bey's warning, even to Özdemir. I wanted to judiciously deflect the question by using complicated medical terms. I think Özdemir realized this, but he did not press the matter. He shook my hand again and said: "Look at me, Afif; you are all honest, reliable people. I believe you and I am happy that I am your friend. However, one last word: count on me for anything, even to put my life on the line. Do not forget that you may share your work and your problems with me!"

I shook the hand of this gold-hearted young Turk with all earnestness; I could not hold back the tears provoked by my intense emotions.

19 September.—Tonight we took turns watching Şadan with Doctor Resuhî. Özdemir was not in the room, but I knew what he was doing. He spent all night walking around the house in the garden. When morning came, we saw how exhausted and haggard the poor girl was. Her gums had receded like a corpse's; her teeth looked sharper. Although when she awoke, her innocent eyes softened her countenance, when she slept she appeared stronger; and sometimes her features resembled a cruel smile. Doctor Resuhî Bey observed all these changes closely. Frankly, she is becoming disconnected from life. We are losing Şadan. In the afternoon I sent a telegram to Turan and two hours later he had come. Now Doctor Resuhî Bey and Turan are with Şadan and I am writing these lines in my notebook. I shall take over the watch from Resuhî Bey in fifteen minutes.

Letter from Güzin to Şadan.

"*17 September.*

"Dear Şadan,

"I know how great my faults are, and you have every right to complain, but I have not been able to find a free moment to write. Let me explain. First, I met my dear husband, my Azmi, at the station, and our dear elder Rıfat Bey was waiting for us with an automobile. He took us to his home above the office.

" 'My children,' he said, 'yes, you are indeed my children. You know that although I have wealth, I have no one else except you. I have raised Azmi as my own son. Güzin, I raised you in part as well, as you were entrusted to me by my closest friend, your father. Since you are now husband and wife, you shall live together and make my last days brighter and happier. In my will I have left Azmi everything. Now, is this situation understood?'

"I began to cry before this good, kind-hearted gentleman while Azmi, with tears in his eyes, kissed the old man's shaking hands. That is how we met with Rıfat Bey. Now Rıfat Bey has a partner, and the two men are busy at the table all day, examining all sorts of business. However, Azmi is still very weak! My poor husband; can you blame me? He has gone through so much pain. But he does not yet wish to speak about his trip.

"How is your mother? I hope her health is better. Give her my regards and love; and give her love from Azmi as well. I have written that Azmi is very weak. Even as I was writing this letter he started out of his sleep, and I went to him quickly to calm him. Of course, our happiness and comfort will put an end to all of this. But you see, I have talked all about myself again. Now let us speak of your news: When is your wedding? Do you see Turan Bey a great deal? Tell me all about it. With much love, my dearest Şadan."

Letter from Güzin to Şadan.
(Unopened by her.)

"18 September.

"My dear friend Şadan,

"We have suffered a terrible blow. Many cold-hearted people may see this as boon for us, but you know very well that this is not the truth. Our surrogate father, the most generous protector of our life and future, Rıfat Bey, passed away suddenly. We do not believe we would be so distraught even if our real fathers were alive and had died. This kind-hearted man left us a fortune that we could never imagine earning. This event has had a terrible effect on Azmi, who was already very weak. I am trying my best to distract him with other, more pleasant things. Oh, dear Şadan; here I am, worrying you with all of my troubles. Forgive me, I cannot help it; I have no one to confide in except you. I will come to see you soon. Goodbye, my beautiful.

"With much love,
"Güzin"

From Doctor Afif's Diary.

20 September.—Only resolution and the habit of many years allow me to continue writing in this journal. I am too miserable; I have lost all hope. If I were to meet my death today, I would feel not the slightest sorrow for the life I leave

82

behind. Death is already floating all around me. Şadan's mother died, then Turan's father; now the unfortunate, sweet Şadan. But let me stop; let me try to record these events while I have them in my mind. As I have said, while Resuhî Bey and Turan were in Şadan's room, I came in to relieve my old tutor, then attempted to send Turan to his room. At first he did not wish to leave; however, when I explained that we would need him tomorrow, he acquiesced. Doctor Resuhî Bey treated Turan with the compassion of a father. He tried to console him, saying, "Come, my child. Come, my son; you are very tired too. Let us go into the other room; there are two sofas there. We can lie down, and our hearts will comfort and strengthen each other."

After a last look at Şadan, her face chalky white as she lay on the bed, he left the room with the doctor. I was alone, and when I looked around I saw that the doctor had arranged everything and had put the garlic flowers in place. The window frames were covered with them, and Şadan wore a chaplet of them around her neck. I looked at her; she was having difficulty breathing. Under the frosted lamp her teeth appeared even sharper than they had been in the morning. It must have been some trick of the light, especially as the canine teeth appeared longer and sharper than the rest. I sat down by the patient; she moved uneasily, and at that moment I heard a noise made by something soft flapping against the window. I went over to it and raised one side of the curtain. The moonlight illuminated the entire scene, and there was a large bat outside the window. It flew away, possibly startled by the light. It began flying in circles and striking the window with its wings. When I came back to the bed, I noticed that Şadan had moved and torn away her wreath of garlic flowers. I replaced them as well as I could, according to Doctor Resuhî Bey's instructions, and observed the patient. Presently Şadan awoke and I gave her food as the doctor had prescribed, but she ate very little. However, it struck me as curious that the moment she became conscious, she pressed the garlic flowers close to her. It was odd: I noticed that whenever she got into that lethargic state, with the stertorous breathing, she put the flowers from her; but when she awoke, she immediately clutched them and put them around her neck. This went on so many times during my watch that there could be no mistake.

At six o'clock Resuhî Bey came to relieve me. When he saw Şadan's face, I again heard that very familiar sigh. With a sharp whisper, he said, "Turn on the lights!" and examined Şadan carefully. He removed the flowers from around her neck, and as he did so he started back, as though afraid. "Oh my God!" he said. I bent over and looked, too, and as I noticed a chill came over me.

The wounds on her neck had completely disappeared!

My old tutor stared at Şadan's face carefully for fully five minutes, and then he turned to me and said:

"She is dying. It will not be long. Now listen carefully, there is a great difference whether she dies conscious or in her sleep. Go and wake that poor boy, your unfortunate friend, so that he may see his lover's final moments. We must let him know!"

I went quickly. I woke Turan, and when he leapt from the sofa and saw the morning light he cried out: "Have I slept too long? My God!" I assured him that Şadan was still asleep, but told him as gently as I could the outcome that both Doctor Resuhî Bey and I feared. Without a word, the poor child put his face in his hands and fell on his knees. His shoulders shook from sobbing. I held his hand gently, saying, "Come, my dear brother; come, we are at a time when we need all of your strength and courage!"

When we entered the room, Şadan opened her eyes, and when she saw Turan she said in a weak voice:

"Turan, my love, how good of you to come!"

Turan was leaning over his fiancée to give her a kiss; Doctor Resuhî Bey intercepted him with a swift motion and said:

"No, not yet. Hold her hand; it will comfort her more!" Turan held that dear hand and knelt beside her bed. At that moment Şadan looked as fresh and beautiful as an angel.

However, slowly her eyes closed and she fell asleep. For a

brief moment she breathed lightly; her chest rose and fell like a tired child's. Then there came that strange change in her face which I had noticed on my watch. Her breathing grew stertorous, the mouth opened, and the pale gums, drawn back, made the teeth appear longer and sharper than ever. She opened her eyes, half-awake, half-asleep; those eyes which a moment before shone like an angel's were now both glassy and hard. With a soft, voluptuous voice that I had never heard from her lips, she said:

"Oh, Turan, my lover, I am glad you have come… Kiss me, kiss me!"

Turan leaned over his lover for a kiss; but at that moment Resuhî Bey swooped upon him like an eagle upon its prey, clutched him by the shoulders with a strength I never thought he could have possessed, and hurled him across the room.

"Do not dare, for your life and the safety of her soul!"

The old professor roared these words and stood before Turan. Turan was so taken aback that for a minute he could not speak. And although a momentary cloud of anger passed over his face, he thought better of it and contained himself. Both Doctor Resuhî Bey and I turned our eyes to Şadan. We saw a spasm as of rage and hatred flit like a shadow over her face; the sharp teeth champed together. Then her eyes began to close and her difficult breathing began again. It was not five minutes later when Şadan reopened her eyes, but this time her face once more had a sweet, angelic glow. The poor girl reached out her thin, weak arm, held Doctor Resuhî Bey's large, dark hands, and kissed them with respect and gratitude. Then, in a faint voice, but with unspeakable pathos:

"Ah, a true friend to Turan and me!" she said. "Protect and comfort him!"

The old professor knelt beside her, and in a deep and majestic voice said:

"I swear it!" He then turned to Turan: "Come, my son, take her hand and kiss her on the forehead, but only once."

Turan kissed his lover's forehead, and Şadan's eyes closed slowly. Resuhî Bey, who was now watching Şadan, held

Turan's arm and took him outside. When he returned, her breathing became more stertorous. Then, suddenly, it ceased. The old doctor, in a faint voice, said:

"It is all over… She is dead!"

When I opened the door, I saw Turan on his knees, sobbing. I hurried back into the room. Resuhî Bey was examining her face with a stern and grim expression. How strange! Death had returned this poor girl's beauty. Her face and lips became pink and almost rejuvenated. I stood beside the professor:

"Poor child," I said. "At least she finally found peace; her suffering has ended."

The professor shook his head solemnly:

"Not so, not so! We are at the beginning of pain and trouble."

I asked what he meant, and he only said:

"We can do nothing as yet. Wait and see."

CHAPTER VIII

FROM DOCTOR AFİF BEY'S DIARY—*continued.*

A strange thing: Doctor Resuhî Bey's behavior has taken a mysterious turn. In particular, the look he gave the poor, gentle, innocent Şadan after her death appeared almost spiteful. Of course, I could not expect Resuhî Bey to shed many tears, since he had not loved this precious girl as I had. However, although the old professor behaved strangely from time to time and held some fantastical beliefs, he now became even more peculiar.

After Şadan and her mother's funerals, Resuhî Bey said in a grave and thoughtful tone:

"We will make ourselves comfortable tonight. Unfortunately there is nothing to be done for now, but tomorrow afternoon you will bring me a set of post-mortem knives. And no one must hear of the things I shall tell you."

"My dear tutor, what must we do now; will we perform an autopsy?"

"Yes and no! I wish to operate, but not as you think. I shall cut off Şadan's head and remove her heart!"

I thought Doctor Resuhî had suddenly gone mad. He continued with great conviction and composure:

"Look at that, you are among the bravest surgeons, and yet so shocked, eh? You even tremble. I am sorry, my friend Afif, I had forgotten that you loved this poor girl. However, you shall not perform the operation. I shall, and you must only help. In fact, I would like to do it tonight, but for Turan's sake I must not. He is busy just now with his father's funeral. Yet it is also necessary that he not see Şadan. Ah, if only it were possible to open the coffin secretly and perform the operation now."

I still thought that I was dreaming or that the old professor had gone insane. I said angrily:

"But why do it at all? The girl is dead and gone. Why would you mutilate a poor woman's body in such a horrible way? If it will do no good to her or to science, it is monstrous."

The professor interrupted me quickly:

"My friend Afif, I pity your heart, wounded by sorrow and love. I respect your feelings. However, there are so many things that you do not know. You shall learn about them when the time comes, and although they are unpleasant, you will thank me. Afif, my son, you have worked and lived with me for many years, and yet did you ever see me do anything foolish, against conscience or law? Let me remind you of a small incident: when I prevented Turan from kissing Şadan as she was about to die, you were angry with me. But did you not see how Şadan thanked me for it with her beautiful eyes and her weak voice once she regained consciousness? Did she not kiss my hand and commit Turan to my protection? You have believed in me for many years, trusted me throughout this strange and horrible incident. Now, my child, I want you to continue to trust me for a week or two more!"

He stopped for a minute. Then he continued solemnly:

"My son Afif, there are strange and terrible days before us. Let us not be two, but one, so that we may work toward a good end. Will you not have faith in me?"

I took the hands of my dear tutor, whose good intentions I did not doubt. I kissed his hands and, withstanding intense emotions, promised that I would listen to him and trust him.

The next day Turan called before noon. The grief over his father and lover had had a noticeable effect on this young man, who was as strong as a rock! A few moments later, Resuhî Bey also joined us and we dined at my home. The old doctor had the compassion almost of a father for Turan. After a short time, the bond between them had grown even stronger. At dinner the doctor said to Turan:

"I know you were very angry at me for preventing you from kissing Şadan; however, both you and I were correct. You could not have trusted me and I could not have acted any other way. But one day I shall ask for your absolute and total trust. Prepare yourself for that moment. Later you shall thank me, both for your own sake and for the sake of your loved one. Remember that Şadan has entrusted you to my protection. In these times the gates of the truth are opened to those who are soon to meet with death.

"From now on, you are a son to me like Afif. We all knew the Major Turan Bey who rose to fame in the epic victories of our national struggle in Anatolia; but now I ask for the right to call you simply 'Turan,' as though you were my son."

Turan sprung from his chair and respectfully bowed over the still-strong hands of the professor. Resuhî Bey continued in a manner that I did not understand:

"Turan, I was just telling Afif that we have gone through a great deal. Especially you; you are in a more agonizing position than either of us. However, there are more evil and painful days—and more heartbreaking episodes—ahead of us. But if we walk together to the end, we will see the light at the end of the tunnel."

I almost forgot to write here: Doctor Resuhî Bey told me privately that the surgical knives would not be necessary for the present.

From Güzin Hanım's Diary.

20 September.—How short the time has been since the first entry in my journal. Much has happened, good and bad, between these dates. When I wrote those first lines, Azmi was on his accursed trip to Transylvania and I was dealing with the sorrow of not hearing from him. Now Azmi has returned, I have become his wife, and dear Rıfat Bey has passed away and been buried. Azmi has taken over as the owner and manager of the business. However, he has still not fully recovered. One particular incident occurred a day ago that put him in bed again. Now I record it in my journal, which has been my confidant in sad and lonely times.

Two days ago, near evening, I forced Azmi to get up from his desk, as the weather was warm and very pleasant, and I took him to Sarayburnu Park, very close to our home in Cağaloğlu, to get some air. I love the high eastern side overlooking the Straits, the Sea of Marmara, Çamlıca, and the Prince Islands, and the beautiful blue currents of the Bosphorus that have flowed for centuries. Sitting there in silence for half an hour refreshes and strengthens the soul considerably. So I took Azmi's hand and brought him there. The garden was quiet. As I gazed at the Marmara currents, Azmi suddenly clutched my arm and muttered, "Oh my God!" I turned my head instantly. His face had turned pale. His eyes were like those of a child who has seen something terrifying. And those hard eyes were fixed on a tall, slim, hawk-nosed man with a black mustache and pointed beard. This man in black was staring intently at a beautiful young girl. He was so focused on the girl that he did not notice us looking at him. Therefore I had the chance to observe him for some time. His face was hard, cruel, and—how should I put this?—almost lustful. His excessively red lips made his teeth appear even whiter, and they were pointed like an animal's. Azmi stared at him blankly in terror and amazement; I was afraid the man might notice and said:

"Azmi, do you feel ill?"

Azmi evidently thought that I knew this man as well as he did because he replied:

"Do you see who it is?"

"I don't know him; who is it?"

His answer sent a cold shiver through my body, for it was

said as if he did not know that it was me, his wife Güzin, to whom he was speaking:

"It is the man himself!"

Poor Azmi was evidently terrified and excited. For if I had not been supporting him with all of my strength, he would have collapsed. At that moment, the young woman or girl saw some other people and walked to them; and the man followed behind. My husband's look of fear lingered until the man disappeared. Then he whispered to himself:

"That man is the Count. Count Dracula! But he is younger... Oh my God, if what I saw is true... If this is true! Ah, if only I knew... if I knew..."

My husband was in such a sad state of distress and excitement that I was terribly frightened. We returned home quickly, and I sat him down on a sofa and put his head on my shoulder. A minute later he fell asleep, breathing calmly. When he woke, it was as though he did not remember the incident; he smiled at me with loving eyes and said, "I fell asleep, Güzin; how long I must have kept you waiting." It makes me so sad that Azmi has these episodes of fear and forgetfulness. This may eventually lead to some disaster. I have made a resolution; when I found him in the hospital in Edirne, he gave me his journal and made me promise not to read it unless he permitted it or it was deemed necessary for our happiness. And I have kept it. I have not read it, even though Azmi insisted on saying nothing about his strange journey. Have I the right to read it?

The same evening.—My God, what a terrible tragedy! I just received the news of the death of both Şadan and her mother; I am bursting into tears. I do not have the strength to write any more...

From Doctor Afif's Diary.

22 September.—Silence and loneliness... Poor Turan, he has gone with Özdemir Bey to his mansion in Göztepe. This Özdemir is such a brave and noble fellow! I have no doubt that he is as upset about the terrible death of Şadan as Turan and I are; however, he can hide his feelings very well. It's as though he wears a steel mask. Who need fear for the future of the Turkish nation and Turkish lands when the mountains and highlands of Anatolia continue to raise such lionhearted, pure, and sensitive children? Doctor Resuhî Bey is sleeping in the other room; tonight he will go to Yakacık, stay there one night, and return. He said there are some preparations that only he can make.

Clipping From the "Zaman" Newspaper Published in Istanbul, 25 September.

A VERY MYSTERIOUS EVENT

During the past three or four days, mysterious events near Eyüp have drawn the attention of the public. In this neighborhood, incidents have occurred of children straying from home or neglecting to return from playing. These lost children are all too young to give an intelligible account of themselves to their parents. However, when asked where they went, they say merely that they "played with the beautiful lady." The children always seem to disappear in the evening; two have been found by their parents the following morning. Police had to become involved. It is strange that they speak of a "beautiful lady." However, police suppose that the children picked up the phrase from the first child and used it as occasion served. There is, additionally, a more serious and important aspect to the story. According to our correspondent and the police report, all of the missing children have been slightly torn or wounded in the throat. These wounds resemble the bite of a small animal like a rat or small dog. The children also showed visible signs of exhaustion. The municipality is conducting a rigorous search around Eyüp for stray dogs.

One last piece of information has reached our newspaper while awaiting publication: A child, lost yesterday evening, was found under a cypress tree in Eyüp cemetery. This child also had the same tiny wounds as has been noticed in the other cases. The poor child appeared to be so exhausted that he was unable to move. He appeared weak and emaciated, as though he had been through an illness in one night. This boy also said that he had been lured to the cemetery by "a beautiful lady."

CHAPTER IX

FROM GÜZİN HANIM'S DIARY

24 September.—I finally read Azmi's notebook from start to finish. My God… How horrible, how horrible! Whether it be true or only imagination, my poor Azmi must have suffered a period of hellish torture. Can such things ever be real? Did he write these long pages during a period of brain fever? It is impossible to discover; for his own mind and health I dare not broach the subject with him. But what of the man we saw in Sarayburnu Park yesterday? Did he not appear to be one hundred percent certain that the man was the Count? Does he believe what he saw and wrote? No doubt; is it not in his notebook that this Count would come to Istanbul? My God, will we face some inconceivable incident, some real and unprecedented catastrophe? Could it be that those awful, frightening stories that we heard as children from Rumelians and our nannies are true? Can this monster be in Istanbul? Ah, Azmi, so many things I would ask him if he were recovered from this mental illness!

Letter from Doctor Resuhî Bey to Güzin Hanım.

"24 September.
(Confidence)

"Dear Madame;

"I beg your forgiveness for bothering you like this. Because I have been responsible for the treatment of Şadan Hanım and have been empowered by both her fiancé and her poor mother, I have read Şadan Hanım's letters and diaries. In them I have encountered stories of how close a friend you were to the deceased. I ask for your information to prevent great, inconceivably large catastrophes and to save some of your loved ones from pain. You may believe and trust me, for I am a close friend of Afif Bey and Turan Bey, fiancé of the deceased Şadan Hanım whom you loved very much. When and where may I see you? I beg your forgiveness again. I understand very well from the letters you wrote to Şadan Hanım that you have a golden heart and character. I am also aware of your husband's illness; perhaps it would be better to keep our meeting private to avoid upsetting him. With all my respect."

Telegram from Güzin Hanım to Resuhî Bey.

"25 September.

"Please come today, we can meet any time.

"Güzin"

From Güzin Hanım's Diary.

25 September.—I cannot help feeling terribly excited as the time draws near for the visit of Doctor Resuhî Bey. I expect that it will throw some light upon Azmi's horrible adventure. I will also learn more about my poor friend from this man, whose name I have read in the newspapers, whose work I have heard of, and who treated Şadan. Of course the doctor is coming to ask me about Şadan's sleepwalking; however, Azmi's diary, which was full of such horrible things, gets hold of my imagination and makes me feel as though everything is connected with it.

Luckily Azmi will be away from home today to take care of some important business. The doctor and I may speak as we wish.

The night of that day.—Resuhî Bey has come and gone; oh God, what a strange meeting! My head is spinning. I feel like I have lost my mind. It is as though I am in a nightmare. My God; can these things, even a small part of them, be true? If I had not read Azmi's diary first, I should never have accepted even the possibility of what Doctor Resuhî Bey has told me. My poor, dear Azmi! I understand very well now what horrible suffering you have endured. My greatest wish is for all of this not to upset him again. But even if it does, it may be a consolation to know for certain that his eyes and brain did not deceive him. Who knows? Perhaps his current misery is caused by self-doubt. This Doctor Resuhî Bey is a strange person— not strange, but eccentric. I can now better understand the rumors about him in the press. However, I find it very odd that his generosity and great compassion for all mankind are not understood by everyone. When he abandons that rigid, dry, scientific exterior, he gives the impression of a compassionate father. When he sat in front of me today, without waiting for an offer or asking, he at once began:

"Güzin Hanım, I ask you again to forgive me and will come straight to the point: I have read all of the letters you wrote to poor Şadan, with permission and the curiosity given by my profession. Apart from these, Şadan also occasionally kept a diary after you left; I have read and examined this as well. It mentioned her sleepwalking and that you once rescued her. Now I ask you to tell me all you can remember about that."

"Doctor, there is no need to remember. I have written it all in my diary as it happened; allow me to show you."

I spoke these words and gave him the section of my diary which I had written out on the typewriter in the office. Since I had guessed that the doctor would ask about it, I had typed out the sections pertaining to Şadan in advance. When I explained this to Resuhî Bey, his eyes sparkled.

"Congratulations, Güzin Hanım; you have a rare business mentality that is unfortunately absent in many young women. Your husband Azmi Bey must consider himself lucky to have you."

Then he sat down on the sofa near the window and began to read the papers as though he had forgotten the rest of the world existed. When he had finished, he said:

"Güzin Hanım, there is great darkness in this world, but also light. You are one of the lights. Reading the letters you wrote to Şadan and the passages from the diary you have been kind enough to give to me is enough to understand you. You are one of the lights and angels of this world. I congratulate Azmi Bey again. Forgive me, the importance of the job on my hands is making me forgetful. How is the health of your husband for whom, even though I do not know him personally, I have come to feel a deep and pleasant affection? There is a good chance that he may also have important and helpful thoughts on this matter."

It was now the time to confess the deep, inconsolable pain in my heart: my concerns about Azmi's health and spirit. To this great expert on mental and psychological health, I said:

"He was very well recently, but I think Rıfat Bey's death has affected him, for he became worse the other day in the park."

The doctor interrupted:

"Yes, I know that Rıfat Bey is dead; I have also read the last letters you wrote to Şadan on this subject. But what is the new incident? In what ways has he become worse? I may be able to offer an opinion if I knew these things."

"In the park, Azmi thought he saw a man connected with an incident that caused his mental breakdown and left him with horrible memories."

At that moment I stopped. I did not want to talk anymore; however, the whole thing overwhelmed me in a rush. The worry and the concern I had for Azmi, the crushing uncertainty torturing my poor husband, the mystery surrounding his diary, the maddening fear that has been brooding over me ever since, and a hellish doubt of "what if" all came in a tumult. I do not know how or why, but I found myself kneeling before Doctor Resuhî Bey, reaching for the hands of this white-haired, strong man who inspired feelings of respect, courage, strength, and trust. I was imploring to him to save Azmi. The doctor took my hands, raised me up, sat me down on a chair next to him, and said in a deep and soothing voice:

"My life has been barren and lonely. I have been so busy with other things that I have not had time for friendship. However, since I have been summoned to Istanbul by my student Afif, I have known so many good, honorable, and dear people. You are one of those people, my daughter. Rest easy; I will help you and your husband with all of my power and ability. Now, tell me about your husband!"

I had made my final decision; I would tell this old man everything. But I was afraid he would think that I was on the verge of insanity and assume my husband had gone completely mad. When I spoke of my concern, he said in an odd tone:

"Ah, my girl, do not let that worry you. If you only knew how strange is the matter that brought me here, you would laugh at me and call me crazy. But I know this world better than you, and I have learned not to laugh at anyone's private lives or beliefs."

I rose and handed him Azmi's diary.

"Well then," I said, "take this notebook; read it carefully from start to finish, even though it is a bit long, and tell me what you think!"

Resuhî Bey took the notebook, shook my hand with compassion, said simply, "I shall come tomorrow," and went away.

Letter from Doctor Resuhî Bey to Güzin Hanım.

> "*25 September, evening.*

"My dear daughter,

"I have read the diary. Strange and and terrible as it is, it is entirely true. Have no doubt. I will pledge my life on it. This situation may be horrible for others, but there is no danger for you. Your husband is a brave, tough, and daring Turkish man. I can tell you from experience that not even one person out of a hundred thousand would have been brave enough to climb down that cliff wall and enter the Count's room. In particular, the fact that he had the nerve to go to the crypt for a second time is a testament to his courage and might. Do not worry, your husband's mental health is sound. I can promise you this before I have even seen him. Knowing and meeting with you can only be the great God's blessing to me. I have learned so much from you at once that I am dazzled and confused—more so than ever. I must think, I must think!

"Your eternal and always faithful friend,
"Doctor Resuhî"

Letter from Güzin Hanım to Doctor Resuhî Bey.

"25 September.

"Dear Doctor Bey;

"A thousand thanks for your letter.

"However, if all of it is true, please think, Doctor Bey; that horrible man is in our beautiful Istanbul at this moment! That accursed descendant of the Impaler Voivode of history… I do not know, but it may even be the man himself! The very same man! That bloody and horrible monster. Oh God. Great God! The bloodiest, most terrible and shudder-inspiring march across centuries in history! If you can come tomorrow morning, we can meet when Azmi is not at home."

From Attorney Azmi Bey's Diary.

26 September.—I thought never to write in this diary again. However, events compel me. Last night after supper, Güzin told me that Doctor Resuhî Bey had visited, and that he had read and confirmed everything in my journal. I saw his letter as well. Now I feel quite strong and recovered, and I realize that it was my self-doubt that was killing me. Yes, I have regained my courage and strength; I do not even fear the malevolent Count. So this sinister man is the doppelgänger descendant of that bloody Impaler Voivode. Oh… Perhaps he was finally able to come to Istanbul. So the man I saw was the Count himself! But I wonder how he has become younger. If what Güzin said is true, Doctor Resuhî Bey must be the man to hunt down and destroy this monster.

Evening.—Today I visited Doctor Resuhî Bey. Güzin is quite right, he really is an exceptional character. Pure, strong, kind, wise, and tolerant. He was very happy to see me well. "Güzin Hanım told me that you were very sick," he said. I told him that his letter had cured me completely. We parted ways after setting a date to meet again.

From Doctor Afif's Diary.

26 September.—Alas, everything has been thrown into chaos again. For the last two days I have worked in peace; Turan and Özdemir have been in Erenköy. But as I was sitting in my room, Resuhî Bey bounded through the door and thrust a *Zaman* newspaper in front of my face.

"Tell me, what do you make of this?" He crossed his arms and stood in front of me. A part of the newspaper had been marked with a red pen.

I read the article entitled "Mysterious Event." At first I really did not know what he meant; but after reading the passage about the small wounds on children's throats, I stopped and looked at the doctor. He said merely:

"Well?"

"Just like poor Şadan!"

"Yes, what do you make of that?"

"Simply that there is some cause in common. Whatever injured these children also injured Şadan!"

"That is true indirectly, but not directly."

"Doctor, what are you trying to say?"

I tried to make light of it, but the professor's attitude sobered me. I had not seen the professor so stern and melancholy even during the worst of Şadan's illness.

"Afif, tell me truthfully. Have you never had suspicions about the cause of Şadan's death? Even after all that has happened, and after observing my behavior?"

"Şadan died from massive blood loss!"

"Very well, then how was the blood lost? Where did it go?" Seeing my difficulty in answering, he continued: "Afif, my boy, you are a clever child. You are equipped with all of the weapons of science, but you are narrow-minded! Like many people, you do not let your eyes see nor your ears hear. It is not you alone; most people, even many scientists, would not be able to comprehend what you cannot. However, can you not confirm the existence of physical, material things? Even though I have many different opinions and ideas due to my personal beliefs, I still say that the biggest fault of today's physics and sciences is that they try to explain everything, and quickly reject what they cannot immediately explain. For example, do you believe in souls entering other bodies, the ability to read thoughts, and such things? No? Nor in hypnotism, spiritualism…"

"I believe in hypnotism; Doctor Charcot has explained that pretty well."

Doctor Resuhî laughed at my reply:

"And that is sufficient, yes? The explanation, the explanation; you poor people! You accept hypnotism, but reject thought reading; we see such great achievements today that if people were to have accomplished them a couple of hundred years ago, the Christians would have burned them at the stake and called them sorcerers, while we Muslims would have crowned them and called them prophets or saints. There have always been undiscovered secrets in life and there always will be. Can you claim to know all the secrets of life and death?"

"My dear tutor, tell me more clearly; do you believe that the little wounds on Şadan's throat were made by the same hand or tool or some such thing that punctured the throats of these children? I am of the same opinion."

The Professor raised his head. "No, you are wrong! If only that were so. Unfortunately, no! It is worse, much worse than that."

I stood and cried out:

"In God's name, sir, what do you mean?"

The doctor collapsed, exhausted, into a chair, crossed his hands, and answered:

"The wounds on the children's throats were made by Şadan herself!"

CHAPTER X

For a moment a deep wave of anger shook my body. Forgetting all of my respect and trust in the old professor, I smote the table and said:

"Resuhî Bey, are you mad?"

The professor raised his head and looked at me. The softness and sadness in his voice brought me back to my senses. He said, hoarsely:

"I wish that I was. Compared to the horrible and painful truth, madness would be the lesser of two evils. Ah, my friend; have I not tried up till now to prepare your mind for the truth? You saved my life; why would I trouble you with baseless conjecture of which I was not certain?"

I was embarrassed by my behavior. I took his hands and said:

"Forgive me, master!" He continued:

"You loved poor Şadan; that is why you are prepared to make every sacrifice for her. However, I knew that this concrete truth would be very hard for you to accept. So tonight I will prove it; do you have the courage to come with me?"

The fact that things were taking such a real and frightening shape had frozen me in place. I could not think. My God, what was going on; what was happening?

The doctor continued:

"Now, I will tell you what we are going to do: the two children that were recently found unconscious in Eyüp cemetery are at Etfal Hospital. The head doctor is my friend Hasan Kami Bey, whom you also know. We will visit the hospital and see the children's wounds. Do you know what we shall do if we turn out to be correct? We shall spend the night in Eyüp Sultan, near the family cemetery where Şadan and her mother are buried; I have already acquired the keys to this spacious and protected area."

At that moment I was thinking about the coincidence of Şadan's family cemetery and the children's location both being in the Eyüp Sultan area. I went to Etfal Hospital with the doctor; I examined the children's throat wounds closely. Both were weak from blood loss; their wounds were exactly the same as those upon Şadan. But it was obvious that the teeth or tools that created these wounds were smaller and sharper than those used upon Şadan. I cannot describe the tumult that was swirling in my mind at that moment. I can only say that I felt like a man who had been brought to the edge of a cliff, who was in constant fear of falling. Speaking little to each other, Doctor Resuhî Bey and I left the hospital. I followed him as though hypnotized. After walking a little further through the streets, we took an automobile to the pier. We crossed the Bosphorus to Eyüp Sultan. The dark of night fell over the waters of the "Golden Horn" and the hills of Okmeydanı. Rough, brown, earth-smelling darkness was creeping in from the deep corners of the Bosphorus, Kağıthane, and Silahtarağa valleys, and it filled my heart with an unknown, unexplainable dread. My God; have I been living inside the ring of some horrible truth? Or have I been dreaming? Was there anything in common between the fearful things that I was thinking and what I had been taught as truth and reality?

It was even darker when we arrived in Eyüp Sultan. I walked with the professor in the same silence. Eventually we encountered the wall of one of the Eyüp cemeteries. The old professor climbed over this obstacle with surprising agility. I followed. Resuhî Bey walked with confidence through this deep and creeping darkness. Finally we stopped in front of an enclosed grave resembling a mausoleum. It was well-known that it had belonged to Şadan's family for years. With the key in his hand, Resuhî Bey, who must have had nerves of steel, opened the old, cracked, unpainted door. We both entered; however, the doctor did not forget to draw the door to. Then he took a box of matches from his bag and lit the candle he had brought with him. It was not at all a pleasant scene. Before us were hundred-year-old graves, sarcophagi, and stones of different types and shapes such as flowers and turbans.

The old doctor stood in front of a very thick marble coffin—a woman's. This belonged to one of Şadan's great-grandmothers. In this family cemetery there were no separate graves for Şadan and her mother; the coffins were placed in one of the sarcophagi as had been the old tradition. We were standing in front of the sarcophagus containing Şadan's coffin. Presently Doctor Resuhî Bey went over to a dark corner of the room; he bent down and picked up an iron bar which I understood he had hidden there earlier. Then he set a three-or-four-spans-wide piece of thick oak wood, which was also left amidst the sarcophagi, against the edge of the sarcophagus to serve as a slider. I was staring at him, confused. But it finally dawned upon me. I asked, trembling:

"Teacher, what are you going to do?"

"What am I going to do? I am going to open Şadan's coffin to convince you!"

At that moment he pushed on the end of the bar, which he had carefully wedged under the sarcophagus, and used it as a lever to slide the lid over to the thick plank of wood he had placed before. Şadan's mahogany coffin was exposed. Seized with great heartache and fear, I wanted to stop the doctor. However, he persisted. After a minute, the lid of the coffin was open too. Holding the candle inside the coffin, the professor grasped me with his strong hands. I looked inside... but the coffin was completely empty!

You can imagine the effect this had on me. However, the doctor did not appear surprised. I felt inclined to challenge him in spite of the suspicious facts laid before me. I said:

"Yes, Resuhî Bey; I am satisfied that Şadan Hanım's body is not in this coffin. But what does that prove or tell us? This only proves that her body is not here!"

"Indeed, that is sound logic, but it is flimsy! Tell me, why is the body—Şadan Hanım's body—not here?"

"I do not know. Perhaps someone stole it; perhaps they sold it to an anatomical business!"

I also felt the weakness of my conjecture. But there could not be another plausible explanation. In reply, professor Resuhî Bey sighed.

"If only what you said were true," he said. "However, the reality is otherwise; let us go, onto other evidence!"

With my assistance he replaced the lids of the coffin and sarcophagus. He blew out the candle in his hand. We opened the door of the mausoleum and went outside. The professor locked the door, put the keys in his pocket, and then at his request we waited on either side of the cemetery.

I was able to see the tree the professor was hiding behind from the cypress tree where I was concealed. This was simultaneously a monotonous and sober vigil. We had been in worse situations during the Struggle for Independence. But I could not recall a moment that oppressed my soul so much as this one. The hours elapsed; midnight had passed long ago. My body was numb; my nerves were at first excessively tense but eventually calmed completely. I was beginning to feel angry at my tutor and guilty for being so foolish. I do not know how many centuries passed in that state. On a whim, I turned around; I thought I saw a slim, white ghost moving near the trunks of the dark cypress trees. At the same time, a black shadow appeared behind the tree where Resuhî Bey was hiding and advanced upon that white phantom. This was evidently the doctor. However, I had to run around some of the headstones to get there myself. I stumbled over graves without tombstones or rocks. As I moved in that direction, following Resuhî Bey's earlier instructions, somewhere far off a rooster crowed. And again I saw a fast-moving white specter; something like a shrouded corpse passed me, almost flying toward Şadan's family grave. But since trees obstructed my view of the mausoleum, I could not quite see where this white figure entered. When Professor Resuhî Bey saw me, he held out before me the body of a small child and said in a somber voice:

"Do you believe it now?"

With an anger and obstinacy that I could not suppress at that moment, I said, "No!"

Resuhî Bey asked, a little impatiently, "Is this not a child?"

I replied in the same harsh tone. "Yes, this is a child… But where did he come from? And let us see if he has any wounds." The professor appeared to be running out of patience. He struck a match; there was nothing resembling a wound on the child's neck. When I said, triumphantly, "I was right, was I not?" the doctor merely replied, "Thank God we arrived in time!"

We left the child near the Eyüp police station. As we quickly withdrew, we heard the police guard say, "Hey, what is that?"

I write these lines at home. My head aches. I do not know what to say. But I shall try to sleep because Doctor Resuhî insists that we must do this thing again.

27 September.—I met Doctor Resuhî Bey in Eyüp an hour before sunset. The doctor is a very stubborn man; although I have told him repeatedly how illegal and morally reprehensible what we have done is, he still compelled me to return to that same family mausoleum, in broad daylight no less, in indifference to my words. I thought it useless. Şadan's body was not in the grave nor in the coffin. So what good was it to put ourselves in danger again?

We entered the cemetery just before sunset. There is no need to prolong this account any further; this time, when I opened the coffin with the doctor, chills rushed through me.

Şadan's body lay in the coffin as lovely and vital as the day before her death! In fact, she was even more attractive and beautiful than I saw her before. I almost could not believe that she was dead. Her lips were fiery red. On her cheeks fluttered the pink of fresh roses. As I turned to the professor in fear and amazement, he said: "Are you convinced now?" and in a motion that sent cold shivers down my spine, he pulled back her lips and showed me her teeth.

"You see, the teeth are even sharper!" Then he touched the canine tooth and the one below it and said: "And with these, you bite little children and drain their blood! My friend Afif, do you believe it now?"

The feeling of disbelief and resistance to something that was against all the scientific evidence and understanding of the last century resurfaced in my mind.

"What if," I said, "someone came here at night and placed the body here?" The doctor laughed mirthlessly.

"Who would do such a thing, and why? And consider the fact that it has been a week since Şadan's death. How could she remain as fresh as a daisy?"

I had no answer for this. But the professor did not notice my silence; he was opening her eyelids and examining her teeth as though he were working on a cadaver in the morgue. A moment later he turned back to me and, with that same decisive and nonchalant manner he adopted when he lectured me years ago, said:

"I have considered every scientific possibility. I have studied and compared every known history, social event, belief, and legend. I have an ongoing interest in the historical and contemporary beliefs common among different nations. Thus, I consider myself knowledgeable on the subject. Now listen, we have in front of us a dual life—or to be precise, two different lives. Şadan was bitten by a thing the Rumelians called a "Vampire"—it is interesting that it means the same thing in both West and East—and called a 'Cadı'[6] or 'Hortlak'[7] in our

---

6   Witch

7   Ghoul

language. What is it, Afif? Do not be impatient. Yes, you do not know the painful thing yet. But you shall learn soon enough. Although they become a vampire when they are bitten by a vampire, while in this trance-like state they do not receive all of the accursed attributes of that monster. For them, (I do not know if the doctor was drifting here into his famous Sufism beliefs again?) there is a chance of reaching God's presence or, at least, to become the harmless dead and find eternal peace. For this reason I now must kill Şadan one more time; for the peace of humanity and to set Şadan's soul free once and for all!"

My hands were shaking; I was motionless and uncertain. The doctor sensed this and asked: "Do you believe now?" I put my hands against my temples, and as I pressed on them as though I were trying to crush my head, I said:

"My tutor, my tutor! Do not press me! Perhaps, perhaps I will believe it; I am afraid I do… but how will you do what you have said?"

The doctor assumed his scholarly air:

"Afif, my son, you are a true Istanbulite. If you were a Rumelian or had dealt with the stories (folklore) of Trabzon and its surrounding areas, or even had spoken with people who came from the Rumeli and Skopje regions regarding these subjects, you would know the words 'cadı' and 'hortlak.' Or, at least, you would have some information regarding 'humanity's primitive history.' And you would understand that there were societies known as 'cadıcı'—note that the word 'cadı' is used incorrectly in this context—and 'hortlakçı' to fight against what had been generally been referred to by Rumelians as vampires.

"Afif, my son, there is one thing I find strange: my father. He is from Of, a 'wise man from Of,' or a wise 'hodja'[8] as it meant ten years ago; my mother is a genuine Istanbulite. As their son, I am a true Turk! My father was a marine major in Istanbul. From time to time our relatives would come to Istanbul from our hometown, my father's village. During those nights, in the large room of our home in Kasımpaşa, I listened

---

8   A Muslim teacher or schoolmaster.

to their witch stories. These stories that my cousins told had witches knocking at the windows during raging storms, and everyone would tremble with fear. But do not think that I believed in them, for this was around the 1890s and there were young people who loved science and physics. These people were sent to Tripoli en masse, and I was one of them. However, my knowledge of my country's history and my deep interest in all of humanity, in all of the higher sciences related to medicine, and in strange, unexplained phenomena led me into a particular research adventure. The fact that this belief exists with the same intensity and form in the eastern cities of Turkey, Caucasia, and particularly the Slavic regions suggests either some ethnographic conclusion or something even more significant. For in all of those countries, the same solution that I know to be correct was used against vampires and ghouls. Let me get to the point: I am a modern doctor now and I shall use this same solution. I will sever Şadan's head from her body! I will fill her mouth with garlic flowers, drive a stake through her heart, and bury the body."

These words were said about the woman I loved, the delicate and fair body of the woman for whom I turned my whole life into a desert. My soul revolted against this thought. Doctor Resuhî Bey continued speaking as though he had forgotten all this:

"Afif, my son, believing blindly in science is disrespectful to science itself. Science has not been fully explored. There are many things we do not yet know, but which we can see with our own eyes and discuss afterward. Now let us leave here at once."

We put everything back as it was, and the doctor and I sealed the grave carefully. Some time later we were on the road to the Eyüp pier. I was confused, exhausted, and did not know what to think or say. The doctor stopped suddenly and said:

"Afif, I will not be returning with you. I must stay here with my bag. I shall return to the grave and take care of a few things before sunset. Oh, do not panic. I will not do what I have spoken of. I will do that in front of not only you, but also

Turan Bey and Özdemir Bey, to show all of you the terrible truth. I am a man of faith, a religious man, Afif; like many people, I believe that those who have been bitten by vampires and turned into vampires or ghouls themselves will suffer eternally in desperation and tumult, and may bring about an endless catastrophe for both themselves and humanity. However, as I have said before, if the necessary action is taken against ghouls, these unfortunate but incredible things become ordinary corpses. And their souls will earn the eternal rest they deserve. I knew, Afif, that you are a little open-minded and very progressive, and that my words would make you angry; and they did. Unfortunately, they are the truth. And I will prove this to all three of you. What I shall do tonight is nothing but a special experiment, the taking of some measures to stop Şadan—not the angel, but the 'thing' that has had its blood drained and become a vampire—from leaving her coffin."

29 September, morning.—This morning in my room we held a very serious, thrilling, and painful council of war with Doctor Resuhî Bey, Turan, Özdemir, and myself. Doctor Resuhî Bey proceeded to discuss the situation. I forgot my own grief and excitement and began to worry about Turan's condition and his wrath; I was almost trembling. Turan leapt from his seat a few times as though he wished to silence the doctor by strangling him. Özdemir and I also rose. However, the doctor was so sorrowfully, painfully, and terribly convincing that Turan sat down in surprise every time—sometimes patiently, sometimes with defeated rage. Finally Özdemir Bey rose, his face completely white, and said to Turan: "I myself have no doubts about the doctor's words. I am moved by the respect and astonishment I feel toward this kind-hearted scholar." Then he shook the professor's large, brown hands. Finally, Turan also admitted defeat. He put his head between his hands. "Very well, Doctor," he said, "let us go and see, for I am about to go mad!"

CHAPTER XI

FROM DOCTOR AFİF BEY'S DIARY—*continued.*

At fifteen minutes before midnight, the four of us, led by Doctor Resuhî Bey, leapt over the low, dilapidated wall of the Eyüp cemetery. The sky was cloudy and the night was very dark. But the moon occasionally produced areas of illumination as it moved through scattered clouds, only to disappear again. We stood in front of the mausoleum door; the doctor opened it and looked back. When he saw all three of us hesitating to enter for various reasons, he entered the darkness alone and pulled us in. The three of us looked at each other as we walked, and my attention was on Turan. The doctor shut the door, lit a lantern, turned it toward the sarcophagus, and said:

"Afif, we were here yesterday morning. Tell our friends: was Şadan Hanım's body in the coffin?"

"Yes," I said.

"So look at it now!"

Doctor Resuhî opened the lid of the sarcophagus with the help of a lever and the herculean strength of Özdemir, then opened the coffin lid. Not with triumph but with grief, he said to Turan:

"Look!"

Turan took hesitant steps. Then, by the light of the lantern I held at a distance, he looked into the coffin. His face became deathly pale. The coffin in front of him was completely empty!

Among the frozen friends, it was the doctor who broke the silence: "Now, out!" We all exited the gloomy mausoleum into the dark cemetery. The clouds were still chasing each other in the sky and the moonlight penetrated from time to time. The professor was busy closing the door of the mausoleum, and he began to employ himself in a strange way. He took from his bag some items that looked like long sheets of paper, and he glued these to the keyhole, doorway, and any gaps in between with the help of something—probably a glue bottle. The sanest man among us, Özdemir Bey, asked: "What are you doing, Doctor?"

The professor replied soberly: "I am preventing the re-entry of the vampire to this mausoleum. During the day I wrote verses from the Quran on these pages!" This surprise left all of us speechless. Had Doctor Resuhî Bey truly gone mad? Turan raised his hands in anger, but Özdemir held them back and calmed him. When this was over, we waited in the shadows of the trees that the doctor had appointed for us. I do not know how long we waited. But finally we heard the doctor's whisper, deep but sharp as a whistle: "Look!" We all looked where he pointed. Yes, there, between the dark cypress trees and the start of the road now illuminated by moonlight stood a delicate, white shape, like a ghost. We could not see its face, for it was bent down over what appeared to be a very small child. But we could see the profile of a young, dark-haired woman with a white shroud torn at the top. A moment passed, and then we heard a shriek. It resembled the sound of a child having a nightmare. We all started forward. But the professor stopped us with a sharp gesture. At that moment the shrouded figure moved toward us. I felt the blood freeze in my veins. Simultaneously I heard Turan to my left utter a cry as though his lungs were about to collapse. The phantom in front of us was Şadan!

But Şadan's ghost was completely different. That purity and beauty had given way to cruelty; and the familiar shyness on her face was replaced with a frightening lust.

At a sign from the doctor we quickly left our places and formed a line before the door of the mausoleum. Doctor Resuhî Bey raised the lantern and drew the slide without hesitation. When the light fell on Şadan's face, we saw that her lips were crimson with fresh blood and that the stream had trickled down over her neck and stained her shroud!

We all felt a shudder of fear and disgust pass through us, as cold as death itself.

I could see by the tremulous light that even Professor Resuhî's nerves of steel were failing. Turan was next to me, and if I had not held him up he would have fallen.

When she saw us, Şadan drew back and snarled like a dog. Then she glared at us. Her eyes, once kind and deep blue, shining like a morning star, now burned with the fires of hell. A sinister glow wreathed her face. With a careless motion she callously flung to the ground the child who up to now she had clutched strenuously to her breast, growling over it as a dog growls over a bone. As the child moaned piteously, unable to move, Turan uttered another pained cry. With open arms and a wanton, hellish smile, Şadan advanced toward Turan invitingly. I saw the poor young man back away, covering his face with his hands.

However, Şadan continued to advance with an enchanting and weird grace, and spoke with indescribable seductiveness:

"Come to me; come, Turan! My arms are waiting for you; my lips are longing for you; leave them and come to me! Come, my love, come!"

Ah, what kind of magic, what kind of hellish, devilish deception was in that invitation! Turan moved his hands from his eyes as though under a spell. He slowly opened his arms. He advanced toward this sinister, bloody creature from which only a moment before he had recoiled in fear and disgust. Şadan made a quick, joyful move to meet those open arms. But at that moment I saw Resuhî Bey dart out and hold an open book to her face; it was a Quran. The vampire turned away with a hideous growl. Her face was distorted with anger and hatred; she passed by the professor and moved furiously ahead toward the mausoleum.

But we saw this horrible ghoul, this vampire, stop suddenly a few steps from the door as though arrested by an invisible force. A moment later she turned back, and the moonlight clearly illuminated her face. Never could I have imagined such a grotesque, unutterable look of lust, fury, and loathing. Could such a thing exist even if Azrael and Death itself had wished it?

Resuhî Bey hurried toward the door and removed one of the pages that sealed the gap between the door and its hinges. Before we even understood what was happening, we saw Şadan's physical body turn almost into water—no, vapor—and slip through that knife-edge crack!

Then the professor turned to Turan: "Now, Turan Bey," he said, "will you allow me to do as I wish?"

Turan fell on his knees, covered his face with his hands, and cried:

"Ah, Doctor, do as you must. It is horrible, horrible!" Özdemir and I took the poor man by his arms and raised him up. The doctor lifted up the child, who was off to the side, moaning. Deftly, we left it near a police station without revealing ourselves to anyone, despite the danger.

As we parted ways, the doctor said:

"Come to me tomorrow at noon; we will complete our job together in daylight."

Turan and Özdemir stayed at my house. We all lay down on one of the sofas. I do not need to explain the rest.

* * *

All four of us were at Şadan's grave the next day at two o'clock. This time the doctor brought with him a long and heavy leather bag. We opened the coffin with trembling hands. My God; Şadan lay in the coffin with her bloody mouth, neck, and shroud—and her exceptional beauty. And by this time we had almost grown accustomed to this grisly scene. On one hand, we still could not believe our eyes and minds; on the other, we could not find in ourselves the courage to deny the evidence before us.

Although there was still daylight, the doctor lit the lantern he took from his large leather bag to ease the air of gloom and decay inside the mausoleum. On the ground he placed his surgical knives and a thick, polished stake that was about three feet long. After doing this strange thing, he took out a heavy hammer with an iron handle.

The professor looked up suddenly and said gravely:

"Before we get to work, I find it necessary to say a few more things to you. What I shall tell you is about the deeds of these ghouls and the limits of their powers and abilities, which have been researched unceasingly and collected by age-old nations, societies, and some of the tribes who still live throughout the world. I shall explain everything briefly. When a human becomes a vampire, they also face the curse of living in that state forever. These things never die. As the ancients said, they will continue to live over and over and bring new victims and catastrophes to the world. For with the bite of a vampire, all who have their blood sucked by them and die become vampires themselves. And then they prey on other people. So this terror and disaster continues to grow. My dear Turan Bey, had you kissed poor Şadan without minding my interference, or had you embraced her last night, you would have been in danger of becoming the monster that the Slavic people call Nosferatu, Europeans call Vampire, and other nations call Hortlak. Now the exploits of poor Şadan, which you witnessed with grief and fear, are only beginning. The condition of the children whom Şadan has bitten is not yet clear; but if she continues to exist in this vampire form, she will have a constant influence and a terrible effect on them; they will come to her almost willingly to have their blood sucked. However, if Şadan was to truly die, the situation would be resolved. The wounds on the children's necks would disappear on their own. There is another important point that must be considered; when we actually kill Şadan, her soul will be freed from the servitude of evil and she will find eternal peace and happiness. For this reason, the one who will strike the blow of salvation will be doing her the ultimate favor. There is one person among us who has the most right to do this duty, should he wish it."

At these last words we could not help but turn our eyes to Turan. This brave soldier, who did not lose his cheer even when surrounded by death, was now as pale as a ghost. His trembling figure was apparent even in the darkness. However, the poor young man rallied the last of his strength with a superhuman effort and said:

"Tell me, my friend. I shall do whatever is necessary without hesitation!"

Doctor Resuhî Bey said:

"I know, you are as brave as you are patient. But let me tell you one thing: this will take very little time; but once you start, do not falter and do not stop; we shall be there with you." Turan, who with only a little effort was to be the cause of eternal happiness and compassion, repeated in a hoarse voice:

"Tell me, I am ready to do anything."

The old professor came closer to Turan:

"Now take this sturdy stake in your left hand and be ready to put the point over Şadan's heart. Then take this hammer in your right hand. Now, when I begin to read (here the doctor brought out a little book that I later understood was a Quran), you say "Bismillah"[9] and strike the stake over the heart, driving it through until it penetrates to the other side."

From where I stood I saw Turan's face turn completely pale. His hands trembled. But suddenly he plucked up his courage and all of his strength, and now was brave and ready, just as he was instructed. When the holy harmony of the Quran, read by Resuhî Bey's grave voice, began to vibrate in the mausoleum's shadowy corners, Turan put the point of the stake over his lover's heart, raised the hammer, and struck it with all his strength and might.

---

9   "In the name of Allah"

We saw the body in the coffin writhe like a snake. And a hideous, blood-curdling screech came from the half-open red lips!

Yes, the body quivered and twisted wildly. Her sharp white teeth champed together violently and her lips and tongue bled amid the sound of cracking teeth.

Red foam came from her mouth and began to drip down her neck. However, Turan never faltered. My tall friend looked like an incomparable statue as his strong, steady hands rose and fell, dealing heavy blows each time and burying the sharp stake even further into his lover's heart. The horrible quivering of Şadan's body slowly lessened. The champing of the mouth ceased. And finally the body, which had had a small fountain of blood over the heart, became completely still beneath the shroud. The terrible ordeal was over!

The hammer fell from Turan's hands. His large body reeled. Özdemir and I both moved forward to catch him. When we plucked up our courage and looked at the coffin a moment later, we were all frozen in place. The vile, unnatural, hideous color in Şadan's face had disappeared, and the holy light of a calm soul resting in eternal peace had taken its place.

Doctor Resuhî Bey turned to Turan:

"Now you may kiss your Şadan," he said.

With feelings of deep respect, joy, and grief mixed in his eyes, he bent over the coffin and kissed poor Şadan's forehead, which now glowed with the beauty of a pure flower. When Turan and Özdemir Bey left the mausoleum at the doctor's sign, Resuhî Bey severed Şadan's head with a surgical knife. He filled her mouth with garlic flowers. Then we closed the lids of the coffin and sarcophagus and went outside.

After we jumped over the cemetery wall, the old professor turned to us:

"Now, my children, the first part of our journey is complete. We accomplished our first task. However, there is a long road and a difficult trial ahead of us. All that remains now is to find the true author of these disasters we have suffered. I hope, after all you have seen, you will believe me from now on.

When that happens, there arises an objective, a goal; but shall we walk together toward that higher, divine, and altruistic aim? I actually think I have some clues to the real culprit of these catastrophes."

We each took the professor's hand earnestly and told him that we were all with him, even in death. The brave and heroic old man said:

"Very well, we will meet two days from now to begin discussing and investigating this."

CHAPTER XII

As I was leaving tonight, Professor Resuhî Bey gave me two notebooks and said:

"Tonight I must go to Yakacık; this is very important. But a woman I know, Güzin Hanım, is coming here to meet with me. Unfortunately I will not be able to meet her. However, this young woman is very important. Both she and her husband Azmi Bey will be very helpful in our investigation. That is why I want you to meet with them. I will see her here later. One of these notebooks belongs to her and the other belongs to her husband. Before meeting with the wife, read both notebooks very carefully and with an open mind; then you will begin to understand the situation. Afif, my son, we face danger—a terrible, historical one—in these frightening, mysterious times. Güzin Hanım is a very clever and sensible person; you will see this when you speak with her. She was also the dearest friend and the sincere confidant of poor Şadan.

29 September.—I read the notebooks belonging the lawyer Azmi Bey and his wife given to me by the professor; I wonder if what happened to Azmi Bey is really true? Or if this young man who went to Transylvania went mad. My God, what terrible web of secrets are we falling into? In my opinion, the veil of mystery surrounding us is not unraveling. It is becoming even more complicated, unnerving, and baffling.

Güzin Hanım arrived as Doctor Resuhî Bey had informed me. After reading her and her husband Azmi Bey's diaries, her value and importance had increased in my eyes even further. What a beautiful, charming, and thoughtful young woman. In truth, Azmi Bey is a lucky man. During our discussion of Şadan's tragedy, I read some passages from my own diary to Güzin Hanım and she appeared deeply interested. I finally decided to let her read my entire journal. After reading these pages, Güzin Hanım said:

"Your diary is very interesting and very important. I can see clearly that it is one terrible part of a very horrible and unbelievably sad story. Both Azmi and I worked almost day and night after the day we met dear Doctor Resuhî Bey. Today, in the hopes of gathering more information, Azmi went to that place in Bakırköy where Şadan first showed signs of illness and where we know all of the events in the diary occurred. But he will be returning tomorrow. If we keep working together, we will triumph over the most dangerous obstacles!

After a brief pause, she continued:

"Ah, Afif Bey, we will learn even more terrible things; we will confront something that began centuries ago. If only I could tell you what I think is about to happen."

From Güzin Hanım's Diary.

29 September.—My God! Doctor Afif Bey's journal, especially the section regarding Şadan's death, made me very uncomfortable! If I did not know what happened to Azmi in Transylvania I could have never have believed such a thing possible. Something occurred to me; I asked Doctor Afif Bey if his journal had been read carefully by Doctor Resuhî Bey.

"No," he said. "The professor did not need to see this."

However, I am thinking of this difficult, horrible situation we face. To better understand this threat that has been unfolding behind a dark fog for three or four centuries, and which has now stretched its arm to Istanbul, I find it necessary for that fascinating Doctor Resuhî Bey to read Doctor Afif Bey's diary. I think it is essential. Even the smallest detail could help uncover the greatest secrets. My God! I almost see disaster unfolding before my eyes as I write these lines.

When I gave my opinion to Doctor Afif Bey, he was persuaded to show the journal to Resuhî Bey. Turan Bey, Özdemir Bey, Resuhî Bey, and the rest of us will form a council of war, so to speak. By that time Azmi will be back from his investigation in Bakırköy. I have said that even the smallest detail may help to uncover great secrets. One example of this is the fact that Doctor Resuhî Bey and I have read Azmi's notebooks, and we believe sincerely that this horrible creature called Count Dracula, and the coffin of this wild and dark shadow from the Turkish Empire's past, has come to Istanbul from Bakırköy. Who would have thought that a few random lines about a ship with a Russian flag from Varna and crates of soil would yield such results? A vampire in Istanbul… and his identity… Am I dreaming, or am I reading a horror novel?

From Doctor Afif Bey's Diary.

30 September.—Azmi Bey and his wife Güzin Hanım arrived today at one o'clock. I examined very carefully this man who lived a life of hell in the castle of the dreaded Count Dracula. A very polite, but also tough, clever, and athletic young man from Istanbul. He is also good-spirited, just like his wife. But at the same time, he is thoughtful. According to the plan set by Doctor Resuhî Bey, my large apartment has become a sort of rendezvous point. I set aside a room for Azmi Bey and his wife immediately. My private clinic of five or six beds will be very useful for these guests right now. It is really quite fortunate that I do not have many patients.

Late afternoon.—Azmi Bey and Güzin Hanım have put their heads together as husband and wife and are arranging all of the papers in chronological order and by related events, just like expert investigators. I am both envious and amazed by them. According to my private conversations with Azmi Bey, Count Dracula is in Istanbul. He came here from Bakırköy. Through investigation based on the addresses written down by Dracula, Azmi Bey has discovered where they are taking the crates of soil. Azmi Bey already knows the address of the Istanbul house bought in Dracula's name, but he may have bought other places of which we are unaware. I am a complete believer now, too. I am amazed! The truth of recent events is absolutely undeniable. So Doctor Afif believes in ghouls and vampires, eh?

From Güzin Hanım's Diary.

30 September.—I can hardly contain my excitement. Azmi has returned from Bakırköy with very important information. With all our strength we have now declared—yes, I believe we have—war on Dracula, the Impaler Voivode, this vampire from out of the darkness of centuries. When I read our nation's glorious history with tearful eyes, and saw the cruelties and murders committed by this unprecedented monster who had many names, like Dracula, Black Devil, and Impaler Voivode, I cursed myself for not being a Turkish sipahi[10] living 400 years ago. Does this chain of events bring me into the battlefield with that devil in a different way? Strange, very strange! The only person to make all of this right is our brave commander, Doctor Resuhî Bey!

A moment ago, Turan Bey and his assistant Özdemir Bey arrived. Şadan's poor lover, aide, and fiancé, Turan Bey, is a beautiful and kind man. Özdemir Bey is a paragon of the Turkish race and the Turkish type! We all sat and talked while Azmi was present. We discussed what has happened. Then, according to Doctor Resuhî Bey's prior instructions, they read the notebooks of Azmi, Doctor Afif Bey, and myself.

---

10 An Ottoman cavalryman, akin to a medieval European knight.

CHAPTER XIII

FROM GÜZİN HANIM'S DIARY—*continued.*

The night of the same day.—Finally our honorable and fearless leader, Doctor Resuhî Bey, has arrived. When we met two hours after sunset in Afif Bey's large, private lounge, Doctor Resuhî Bey was naturally the chairman of the meeting.

After scanning all of us with his eyes, the doctor said:

"My friends, you have now read and examined for yourselves all of the documents we have. You are also well aware of what has occurred. But now, I would like to give you some information about the characteristics of the enemy we will be fighting. After I have laid these down I will also discuss his history, which will greatly help to set the course of our battle. Yes, my friends, despite what some may say, there are such beings as vampires and ghouls. Almost everyone at this meeting has seen it to be true. In fact, even if we had not the proof of our own terrifying experiences, the writings, stories, and legends of the previous centuries are proof enough. I must confess: I did not imagine the day I would believe in such things. Had I not endeavored to understand the vastness of life, the universe, and the laws of nature—and the fact that our comprehension of them is yet very limited—there would be no way for me to grasp the horrible truth we face. A vampire is not like a bee that dies after stinging a man once. He gains strength as he bites and sucks blood; and his power, abilities, and capacity to work evil increase as he grows stronger. This vampire, who is now among the unknowing people of Istanbul, is the same thing that Romanians, Transylvanians, and Czechoslovakians call Nosferatu; but in this single being is the strength of twenty people like us. He has unprecedented powers of trickery and deception, for they have been honed over centuries. Because he possesses special abilities, he can appear anywhere in an instant and can in certain places create storms and fog. He has the ability to change his form. He has power over some animals. He can grow and become small; he can pass through even the smallest of holes. He can at times vanish completely. This is the abhorrent monster we now combat. Are you prepared to enter into this terrible war?"

At this all the men rose; I did the same. We said that we would not give up fighting, until death, to eradicate this threat to our people and all of humanity. The doctor received our decision, eyes shining, and was gratified. Then he continued speaking:

"My friends, just as these ghouls have unlimited powers, they also have moments of weakness; and there are things that they cannot do. We see indications and rumors of vampires in Ancient Greece, Ancient Rome, France, India, China, and all throughout Germany. All of these common reports and beliefs, as well as what we have seen, tell us that a vampire will live as long as he sucks human blood; he cannot die by the mere passing of time. But he cannot survive without his food: human blood. This creature, which has no shadow like other bodies and can take the form of wolves or bats, has weaknesses, too; the vampire is a kind of chained lunatic. For example, he cannot enter a house without being first invited by someone of the household. But once he enters, he may visit freely whenever he wishes. As soon as the sun rises, all of the vampire's power and strength disappears. If he cannot reach his grave before sunrise, it will end badly for him. But he can change himself during sunset, sunrise, and noon. Furthermore, he can only pass rivers at certain times, and there are some things he cannot go near, like garlic flowers. He is also afraid of the Holy Quran and the soil from the grave of our Prophet. In fact, the Christian nations use their crosses to protect themselves against vampires. In short, the sacredness of religion is considered a weapon against vampires everywhere. If we manage to find the grave of this vampire, we can destroy it. However, the ghoul we face is more cunning and dangerous than any other. Now I will tell you something frightening. My friends, we are about to fulfill a national and historic duty.

"Do you know who this hellish beast is who stands before us? It is none other than the accursed demon known centuries ago to the Turks as 'the Black Devil,' 'the Devil Voivode,' and 'the Impaler Voivode.' To illustrate the extent of this damned creature's ugly, bloody nature, and to demonstrate his conviction, I must detail a few historical events of which you may already be aware. You can see this 'Dracula' in all his bloody, vile color in the pages of history concerning the reign of Mehmed II during the Turkish Empire. This man was born five centuries ago and was responsible for the slaughter of hundreds of thousands of people, and tens of thousands of Turks, near the Danube River.

"Our history, and even his own populace in his day, refers to him as the Impaler Voivode and Black Devil, as we do now. In the pages of our history you may find this demon's family name, Dracula, as well as his given name, Vlad. The Draculas were a great, noble family. Strangely, however, according to Hungarian historical accounts, people believed that members of this family occasionally had dealings with magic and the Devil. In fact, there are still some semi-wild gypsy families today, with no religious beliefs, whose descendants almost worship the Dracula family. In Hungarian and Romanian history, Dracula is also referred to as 'Stregoica,' meaning 'wizard,' and 'Ordoğ' and 'Pokul,' meaning 'the Devil' and 'Hell.' He was given the name 'Impaler Voivode' because he killed all of his Turkish enemies and prisoners, without exception, by means of his horrible and gruesome sentence: impalement. He reserved a large, separate space in his palace in the city and erected hundreds of pikes, for torture, on either side. He used to impale hundreds of poor Turkish prisoners, and then feast and dance in the company of his people amid their screams and wailings. In fact, he was frequently seen to rend flesh from his prisoners' wounds with his teeth, as an hors d'oeuvre, while he continued to drink wine and dance.

"His own people were sick of Dracula as well; his family shuddered with fear because of him. We recognized Dracula as the Wallachian Voivode during the reign of Murad II, and a levy was imposed. In addition, his brother, Rado, had a deep loyalty and commitment to Mehmed II. When Mehmed II took power in the year 865 of the Hegira calendar, the people of Wallachia, his own Christian population, sent a desperate petition explaining that Dracula's terror had reached an unbearable level. Since their situation and his evil intentions were already known, the Ottoman Empire wished to strike this man with the hand of discipline. He did not accept the offer of reconciliation, but crossed the Danube River and the Turkish border with a hundred-thousand-man army he gathered from various other nations. He began to drown Bulgaria in fire and blood, sparing no village, town, or city. Our government not only sent an army against Dracula, but they also sent a light fleet of twenty-five galleys and one hundred and fifty longboats to the Danube, commanded by Yunus Bey. However, this monster Dracula had provided for everything. He was a stubborn and daring warrior. He set traps, defeated the army in a sudden raid, and tore down the light fleet. If you examine the historical records, you will see that Dracula captured both Captain Yunus Bey and the Vidin Keep Hamza Bey, and impaled both of them, leaving them on either side of the Danube River after severing their hands and feet! So Mehmed II went after this man himself. In a most daring move, Dracula sought to make a coup near the Danube. He chose ten thousand elite soldiers who had sworn to die and not turn back, and took an oath himself. He would assault the headquarters of Sultan Mehmed at night, and he would enter the sultan's tent at the outset, either killing him or taking him prisoner during his first strike. The forces under the command of Mehmed II were all deployed to their positions and divided into various units; the forces within the headquarters did not have the numbers to withstand such an unexpected attack. Besides, a raid under such conditions with ten thousand sentinels could have sent an army of a hundred thousand into chaos. Dracula was absolutely certain that he would be successful. With the help of local guides, he approached the Turkish headquarters and launched his assault in the dark.

"This was indeed a terrible and hellish night—an inconceivable catastrophe. Dracula's ten thousand sentinels gathered their forces and attacked what they believed to be the location of Mehmed II's tent, then continued to press onward, slaughtering and crushing sleeping Turks beneath their armor-clad horses. But Dracula was mistaken about one thing. The route he followed crossed the tents of Grand Viziers Mahmut Pisa and İshak Pisa, not Mehmed II; and Turkish soldiers were not the type of people who would easily succumb to the terror of a raid. Enraged by Dracula's audacity but also ashamed that they showed sufficient carelessness to be targeted by a raid, such Turkish beys as Morea Governor Ömer Bey, the son of Turhan Bey; Ahmet Bey, the son of Evranus; Ali Bey, the son of Köse Mihal; İskender Bey, the son of Malkoç Bey; and Ali Bey of the Köse Mihal Bey family stood against the enemy with drawn swords, feeling no need to wear their armor. In the dark of night, an unprecedented, epic battle erupted and lasted until morning. It was not easy to finish Dracula's ten thousand armored sentinels who had sworn to kill and be killed. As the sun rose, the Impaler Voivode's ten thousand heroes fell lifeless to the ground. However, there was almost always a Turk lying near each one. Let me tell you this: the monster Dracula was not among those bodies; he broke his oath to his comrades in arms as he always did, left his devoted company, and ran away.

"Although he was cunning, Dracula was not courageous,

selfless, nor a true hero willing to die for his honor. I will give you one more example to illustrate his bloody and insidious nature:

"Mehmed II sent this man a group of envoys to offer rapprochement. This group was made up of three Turkish beys. When the envoys approached Dracula's hall door, the guards told them to uncover their heads and remove their turbans. These Turks, our brave fathers who bequeathed this country to us with their blood, their swords, and their unwavering heads as a source of eternal pride and sacred value..."

As he spoke these words, Doctor Resuhî Bey lifted his beautiful, courageous head, covered with white hair, which expressed his sober fortitude, and his hands trembled. His wide face and forehead, which always looked a little pale, now became red and flushed with the fire of national pride. We all listened with a sense of awe and peace, like a prophet receiving a divine revelation. Except for Turan and Özdemir Beys; these beautiful and heroic specimens of Turkishness stood up, unable to help themselves. I will never forget the state of these two young Turks for the rest of my life. Two figures, two faces, and two expressions that the most renowned sculptors would not be able to chance upon for years!

Doctor Resuhî Bey continued:

"Yes, our brave fathers could not believe the request made by the Impaler Voivode's commander of the guard when they heard it. Their faces filled with anger, but one of them kept his composure and said:

" 'Look, this request of yours is unfair on three grounds. First, we are Turkish, and the representatives of the Turkish Hakan; your master is the Hakan's vassal. That is why we cannot uncover our heads. Second, uncovering one's head is not an act of respect for Turks. There are gestures that are equivalent; we know them and we will do what is required of us. Third, above all we are ambassadors, and it would be wrong to force us to do something. Go and tell this to your master...'

"At that moment, a second and younger envoy interrupted:

" 'Look; does your master not know that we do not uncover our heads even in the presence of our sultan; indeed that we even enter the presence of Allah with our heads covered? Envoys who are subjects of our Hakan will not uncover their heads!'

"Dracula was, of course, listening to this argument at the door from inside. In fact, he had arranged it. He knew well that Turks would never uncover their heads in his presence. After listening to the argument for some time, he asked for his private guard and instructed him to admit the Turkish envoys as they were. The three envoys with covered heads entered. With the smile of a venomous snake, a viper, upon his face, Dracula sat upon his divan. When the Turks reached the middle of the hall, he roared:

" 'Uncover your heads!'

"Unsurprisingly, the three envoys did not heed this order, and they refused. My friends, then a horrifying scene unfolded that has never before been witnessed in history. This scene was not merely horrifying. It also illustrated the Turkish fortitude and Turkish national honor and dignity, and it had a quality brighter than the stars of the universe and higher than the seven layers of the skies.

"Dracula, the Wallachian prince, and our present enemy of four and a half centuries, who has crawled to us through the passages of time, screamed like a hyena:

" 'If,' he said, 'these Turks love their turbans so much, then nail them to their heads!'

"This was no empty threat. At that moment, guards stepped forward and seized the Turkish men. A group of executioners with one-and-a-half-span-long barge spikes and iron mallets entered the room. Dracula rose, approached the head of the envoy group, and repeated:

" 'Remove your turban!'

"The heroic Turkish bey to whom these words were addressed displayed, in spite of his restraint, a sad smile which drove Dracula mad. Then he screamed:

" 'Strike!'

"Two newly forged nails, held at his right and left temples, were driven into that unwavering head with strokes of the mallets, producing rose-colored fountains of blood that graced the Turkish bey's turban. Then, my friends, the first of these three Turks—the names of whom history, unfortunately, did not entrust to our hearts—fell upon both knees like a glorious, faithful minaret that wanes after finishing its sacred and noble life, instead of turning upside-down in a storm, and fulfilled his final duty to the Turkish nation."

At this point in his speech Doctor Resuhî Bey, this great scholar and teacher, this unique person, this pinnacle of science, enlightenment, and the nation suddenly grew silent. He appeared lost in the glorious history of his country, forgetful of our present situation. He sat down in the chair near him, thrilled and exhausted. We all felt as though he was not with us. He was four and a half centuries away, in the year 366 of the Hegira calendar, and he was with that Turkish bey onto whose head Dracula nailed his turban. No, he was not with him; he was in his soul, in his pain, and in his sorrow— but also in his pride and glory. And this patriotism gripped us all and spirited us away to that mecca of national pride, that miracle of honor, and made us kneel down before it.

I can say that the peace and silent awe that filled the room have not been greater or more sublime in any temple of any religion since the dawn of religion itself.

As though searching for the sharp knives they used against Greeks, Turan and Özdemir Beys looked about them and suddenly said:

"And then?"

Doctor Resuhî Bey rose from his chair and said:

"Gentlemen, why do you ask what happened next? Is there any need to elucidate? The two remaining envoys were Turks as well. Obviously they were given the same ultimatum. They replied bravely as Turks, and one after another, spikes nailed through their brains—brains that were sources of ideals and valor—they died; or rather, they were reborn to live forever. My friends, even though it has nothing to do with our business here, I wish to tell you something. The essence of this unprecedented, legendary event—akin to Roman bravery, and which would make Rome's own Gaius Mucius Scaevola kneel in respect—did not stem from religious faith, which is considered the most powerful of feelings. These three Turkish men who made up the group of envoys knew very well that there is one condition in our religious principles: if your enemy takes you prisoner, and you will not change your religion or will not comply with their demands, and it is certain that they will kill you, then you may appear to submit to this coercion, provided that you keep your moral opinion secret. However, the case before us was not as serious or fundamental as changing a religion; it was merely uncovering one's head, which has no logical or religious significance. But if that is so, then why did these three brave Turks not attempt to take advantage their religion's leniency? Because national pride and the Turkish honor were on the line. Who could doubt the future of nations that hold an unwavering faith in their pride, honor, and nationality? The thing we call 'the ideal' is this faith that we wish to inspire in our youth. It is that faith of national pride that transcended the borders of this monster Dracula's lands, whose undead form we will fight; and it is that faith that made it possible for us to pass through the country of the Teutons, considered the most warlike race and still feared by the world, and allowed the Turkish front lines to see the icy and misty Baltic Sea."

At these words, which sent a thrill through us, Doctor Resuhî Bey suddenly stopped. There were beads of sweat at his temples. He returned to his senses with a motion that looked as though he were attempting to wake from a deep sleep, and he said:

"I think I became overly excited. My intention was to explain the goals of the mission ahead of us and the characteristics of the creature. Yes, the enemy before us is a calculating creature, as I have said. We must determine the method of attack and plan our battle accordingly. We know from the notes in our friend Azmi Bey's journal that fifty crates were prepared in Dracula's castle in Transylvania and delivered by a shipping company to properties that Dracula has purchased by mail. This soil is the fortress of the vampire. In these graves he will lay immobile during the day. These shelters will now be found in different places throughout Istanbul. And aside from the mansion bought through another company, we know of only one of these places. We must capture this monster in one of these graves during daylight, as we did with Şadan, and destroy him. Or, even if we cannot find him, we must make the soil unusable so that we may capture him in the evening or at night in his own form, wandering with nowhere to go. Is it not strange, my friends? We shall prevent a monster, who centuries ago did not tire of drinking Turkish blood, from drinking Turkish blood in Istanbul; and we shall destroy him who could not be destroyed by the armies of any nation. Who would believe it? My God, is it even possible to believe it?"

The doctor ended his speech with those words, which he said almost to himself. Then he turned his aides and said:

"Gentlemen, get to work!"

CHAPTER XIV

1 October, before noon.—The only difficult thing about this horrible situation would have been my dear Güzin's intervention. But my Güzin, delicate as a rose, tender as a hyacinth, turned out to be as tough as steel—no, as tough as a true Turkish girl. Turkish girls… What qualities should be described to differentiate them? The easiest is the pride and enthusiasm she shows when she sees her husband charging against dangerous challenges and obstacles!

Doctor Resuhî Bey, the man who should go down in history, said:

"My friends, we are walking toward a danger greater than you can imagine, and in this fight we need every kind of weapon. Our enemy is not a lone, simple creature. He is at least as strong as twenty or thirty men; he is brave, cunning, and experienced. We have weapons against these things. For example, take one of these small Qurans I am holding and place it close to your heart. Doctor Afif, do not laugh at what I say; do not laugh. Even if it has no effect, the extra 25 grams will not hurt."

Then Doctor Resuhî turned to Doctor Afif Bey and asked, "Are the keys ready?" Afif produced a few newly-made keys.

Then the doctor said, "Let us get to work!" He began walking and we all followed him. I will not go into too much detail. Some time later we were inside the great, old, dilapidated mansion in Balat, near Topkapı. Count Dracula bought this place through correspondence with "A Real Estate Center." After passing through a garden which resembled a jungle, we opened the mansion door and entered, descending a staircase to a dirt basement below the ground floor. The place was dark, and we had to light two lanterns that we had prepared earlier. I held one of them. The deep darkness, which the light of my lantern seemed almost afraid to illuminate, showed a layer of dust over everything. However, the footprints of the carriers who delivered Count Dracula's crates of earth were visible in the dust like tracks in the snow. Since I was the agent of the business office and the intermediary in the purchase of the mansion, I knew the layout well. In fact, when I was in Dracula's accursed castle in Transylvania, I described its interiors to the vampire.

Doctor Resuhî Bey said:

"Children, what we must do now is scour this place and discover how many of the coffins the Impaler Voivode has sent here to use as shelter. This terrible, cunning monster has perhaps not put all of the coffins in the same place, as a precaution. He may have hidden them in other properties that he has bought."

At these words we began to search the basement. Yes, many of the coffins I saw in Count Dracula's castle were here. We counted them; there were only twenty-nine of the fifty coffins.

As we busied ourselves with this, dawn was quickening. Doctor Resuhî Bey said:

"Our first night of reconnaissance has passed without danger. We have the information we needed. It is almost morning; let us get away from here now!"

2 October.—We friends all reconvened. After a long and tiring investigation, we now have the necessary information regarding two more properties Count Dracula has purchased. We even have the interior layouts of the houses. We investigated the carriers without arousing suspicion. That means the great vampire hunt now begins.

3 October.—This Doctor Resuhî Bey is a very calm man. I think that were it not for him, we could accomplish nothing. After we visited the vampire's sanctuary in Eyüp, the doctor told us in the morning:

"Of course you must have noticed that I had a purpose for not destroying the vampire's shelter that night. Had we done anything there, Count Dracula would have guessed that we were onto him and would have taken many different measures to elude us. But now he has no idea what we know. There is a very good chance that the vampire does not know we have the tools to sterilize his soil. Since we learned about the other two properties, and it is possible to get into empty houses without difficulty, we must make the most of this opportunity. From now until this dawning sun sets, the vampire cannot change his shape. I have made a plan of attack."

We were around the breakfast table in the parlor of my house. After breakfast, Resuhî Bey rose and added:

"My friends, at this moment the terrible hunt has begun; we are entering into this awful struggle. We are all armed both physically and spiritually. Our holy books and our pistols loaded with silver bullets are with us as a precaution, and I have all the necessary equipment in my large bag. Güzin Hanım, do not worry and do not lose hope. You will stay here and wait for us. I wish your heart peace."

However, dear Güzin was excited. Although she was greatly worried about my friends and myself, she had great courage and wished to join us. I knew very well that she wanted to do battle with the enemy of her race, the vampire Impaler Voivode. But it was impossible.

So we departed my home, leaving her in that state. An hour later we were in the house in Eyüp Sultan where we had gone the other day. This time, we first searched the entire house at

Resuhî Bey's request. His goal was to find something like a notebook or any special papers that belonged to Count Dracula. But we found no such thing. Then we went into the basement. Here the twenty-nine coffins were just as we had seen them last. Doctor Resuhî Bey said:

"My children, the first thing we will do is sanctify the earth inside the coffins so that the vampire cannot stay here."

Then he took off his jacket. He began to remove the lids of the coffins one by one with a small lever, chisel, and adz. We assisted him. Then the doctor opened his bag again, removed some large sheets of paper with verses from the Quran typewritten on them, and carefully placed these inside the coffins and on the soil. Afterward he also mixed in garlic flowers. Then he ordered us to close the lids of the coffins that had been treated. When we had finally repeated the process for all twenty-nine coffins, they were all boarded up just as they had been before. A few moments later we were out on the street, leaving the house and the garden.

Doctor Resuhî Bey said in a full and cheerful voice:

"It is done. Now there is no way for the vampire to take shelter here. If we are successful in the other two nests, we shall save Turkey and the world from a secret catastrophe. The ghoul is not here today; now, on to the house in (....)!"

4 October.—I must complete the missing parts of my account and close the final chapter of my journal and this horrible disaster once and for all. I believe that no matter how hard I try, I will not be able to write the last chapter in such a way as to reproduce all of its thrill and terror. These lines will be only a faint memory of the final scenes of this tragedy.

As I have mentioned earlier, after making the coffins in the house in Eyüp Sultan useless to Dracula, we got into an automobile. We went straight to the second house in (....). The key we had made let us, without raising any suspicion, into a garden full of trees; after shutting the door slowly from the inside, we moved toward the decaying mansion ahead. This was a single story building with three or four marble steps standing on a wide, marble foundation. With a great thrill we climbed the weathered stairs to the outer door. There was now a strong possibility of encountering the vampire Impaler Voivode lying in one of those coffins, for there was only one other place in which he could take shelter, and we knew where that was. After Özdemir Bey put his wide, strong shoulders to the door, both wings opened completely with a rotten cracking noise. We entered. Ah, yes… There they were; the crates with which we were very familiar lay on a marble surface. The doctor, walking in front of us, stopped. He raised his finger and quickly counted the crates. My God! The other twenty-one crates were before us!

A moment later, with a noticeable crack in his voice, Resuhî Bey said hoarsely:

"Look!" We all turned our eyes in the direction he pointed. There, one of the coffins sat with the lid barely open.

At that moment we saw Turan Bey leap in that direction like a tiger. Özdemir Bey ran after him. We also began running instinctively to protect our friend who was rushing toward this terrible danger. The moment he reached the coffin, Turan Bey lifted his foot and with a kick knocked the lid to the marble floor of the hall.

Count Dracula, the Impaler Voivode of history, this monster from hell, lay on soil that gave off a disgusting odor! His face was as pale as a wax statue but those crimson eyes which I knew too well seemed to burn with a ghastly light.

Even Doctor Resuhî Bey seemed to be caught up in a sudden rush of thrill and horror. However, at that moment something very unexpected happened. With the speed of lightning Turan Bey suddenly produced from under his coat a huge broadaxe. I saw the axe land on the Impaler Voivode's neck with a merciless blow and sever that vile head from its torso. Then another streak of lightning flashed before my eyes; Özdemir Bey drove his long Dagestan knife into the vampire's heart, all the way to the hilt.

I heard Turan Bey utter these words in a faint voice:

"This is revenge for my impaled brethren along the Danube

River, and my Şadan!"

And then we witnessed another miracle. Yes, without believing our own eyes, but with absolute certainty, we saw this happen:

As we watched the scene before us with our eyes wide open, the body and head slowly crumbled to dust, mixed with the dirt, and disappeared!

THE END

AFTERWORD

by Iain Robert Smith

Jonathan Harker's journal famously begins with an account of his journey from London to Transylvania as he describes his experiences crossing the river Danube and entering "the traditions of Turkish rule." This fleeting reference to Turkey within Stoker's original novel is transformed in *Kazıklı Voyvoda/The Impaling Voivode* into an equivalent passage in Azmi's journal celebrating the babbling of the river as "a living testament to the glorious past of the Turkish nation, my great and famous race." These words are the first hint that Stoker's novel was adapted and transformed by Ali Rıza Seyfi in a manner much more radical than *Kazıklı Voyvoda*'s reputation as a Turkish translation of *Dracula* might imply. Indeed, I must admit that for many years I had assumed that Seyfi's novel was a relatively straightforward translation of Stoker's novel into Turkish that had altered some locations and character names but made few substantive changes. When I first heard from Ed Glaser that he intended to have the novel translated back into English, I found it quite a curious idea. What would be the merit of having a version of *Dracula* that had been translated into Turkish and then back into English? How foolish I was.

Obviously, there are many passages here that reproduce

Stoker's novel with only minor variations in phrasing. A close textual comparison shows that much of the novel was translated directly into Turkish and therefore the back translation into English produces quite an uncanny effect as we recognize anew these classic passages with only minimal differences. Nevertheless, it is the more substantial additions that Seyfi made to the text that are the most fascinating and invaluable for our understanding of the transnational legacy of *Dracula* and processes of cross-cultural adaptation more broadly. Collaborating with Necip Ateş to translate the novel back into English, Glaser has done us a significant service by bringing this adaptation to an English-language readership. Part of the reason that this is so important is that the few times that Seyfi's book has been discussed in English-language criticism have been in relation to its film adaptation *Drakula İstanbul'da* (1953) and these mentions tend to show little knowledge of this source text. David J. Skal, for example, explains in *Hollywood Gothic: The Tangled Web of Dracula from Novel to Stage and Screen* that "the only straight-faced adaptation of Dracula made anywhere in the world after 1931 was a 1953 Turkish oddity called *Drakula Istanbul'da*"[1] but he makes no reference to Ali Rıza Seyfi's novel. Meanwhile, Lyndon W. Joslin in *Count Dracula Goes to the Movies: Stoker's Novel Adapted, 1922-2003* discusses the various ways in which *Drakula İstanbul'da* is faithful to Stoker's novel, yet makes only a fleeting mention of "a Turkish novel titled *Kazıklı Voyvoda*" referred to in the film's credits.[2] Of course, these absences are perfectly understandable given that it is only now that Seyfi's novel is available in an English-language translation, but it is equally clear that scholarship is going to greatly benefit from its increased accessibility.

When we compare the novel to its film adaptation *Drakula İstanbul'da*, this value to scholarship is even more pronounced.

---

1 David J. Skal, *Hollywood Gothic: The Tangled Web of Dracula from Novel to Stage and Screen* (Faber & Faber, 2004), 246.

2 Lyndon W. Joslin, *Count Dracula Goes to the Movies: Stoker's Novel Adapted, 1922-2003*, 2nd edition (McFarland, 2006), 47.

Directed by Mehmet Muhtar and produced by Turgut Demirağ, who had previously collaborated on *İstanbul Geceleri* (Nights of Istanbul, 1950) and *Tanri Sahidimdir* (God Is My Witness, 1951), the film was made well before the heyday of Yeşilçam adaptations in the 1970s when Turkish filmmakers such as Hulki Saner and Kunt Tulgar would produce numerous reworkings of globally popular texts including *Star Trek* (*Turist Ömer Uzay Yolu'nda/Ömer the Tourist in Star Trek*, 1973), *The Exorcist* (*Şeytan/Satan*, 1974) and *Superman* (*Süpermen Dönüyor/Superman Returns*, 1979). However, it was nonetheless part of a brief earlier cycle of films in the mid-1950s in which popular film characters were transplanted to Istanbul, with Tarzan appearing in Orhan Atadeniz's *Tarzan İstanbul'da* (Tarzan in Istanbul, 1952) and the Invisible Man appearing in Lütfi Akad's *Görünmeyen adam İstanbul'da* (The Invisible Man in Istanbul, 1955). With a script from Ümit Deniz who would subsequently establish a successful career as a crime novelist and with prolific actor Atif Kaptan in the title role of Dracula, Muhtar's film sticks relatively close to the plot of the original Stoker novel and contains some elements which did not appear in earlier screen Draculas such as a sequence in which the Count walks down the outer wall of the castle, and a scene where Şadan (the Turkish equivalent to Lucy) carries a baby into her tomb, only to drop it when confronted by Doctor Resuhî (Van Helsing) and his team. Of course, these moments are less a marker of fidelity to Stoker's novel than to Ali Rıza Seyfi's adaptation, especially given that the film retains all the character names from Seyfi's version. As Kim Newman noted in the foreword, though, it is important to remember that the film does not follow Seyfi's novel in all respects. The shift in setting from the 1920s to the 1950s means that the film reflects the substantial changes in Turkish society between the 1928 novel and its 1953 adaptation, and Güzin (Mina) is transformed from the relatively demure character of the novel into a cabaret dancer—allowing the film to include numerous opportunities for actress Annie Ball to dance for the audience, including a sequence towards the end of the film where she performs a private dance for Dracula while under his influence. Meanwhile, a hunchbacked servant seemingly modeled on the Fritz/Ygor character in the Universal *Frankenstein* films is added, and the eventual killing of Dracula is undertaken by Azmi alone in the Kasımpaşa graveyard rather than by Turan (Şadan's lover) who beheads Dracula with an axe in Seyfi's novel. Muhtar's film also adds a comedic epilogue scene in which Azmi is frantically disposing of bulbs of garlic, explaining that now Dracula has been defeated he no longer wants them anywhere in his home, obliging Güzin to ask sadly if that means they can no longer eat "garlic in stuffed aubergine."

The most notable differences between Muhtar's film and Seyfi's novel, however, are not these elements that Muhtar added but instead what he neglected to include. Stoker's original novel contained two brief references to the "Voivode" Dracula and Muhtar's film makes this link to the historical Vlad III (Vlad the Impaler) somewhat more explicit, but it is remarkable just how much further Seyfi's novel goes in developing that link between the historical Vlad Dracula and Stoker's fictional creation. From the very first pages of his journal, Azmi is making a connection between Count Dracula and the "bloody, horrible, bloodcurdling acts that Voivode Dracula committed during the reign of Mehmed II in the history of the Turkish Empire" while Güzin's diary later describes how she "read our nation's glorious history with tearful eyes, and saw the cruelties and murders committed by this unprecedented monster who had many names, like Dracula, Black Devil, and Impaler Voivode." Count Dracula is positioned as a foreigner speaking in accented Turkish resembling "that of some of the Greek doctors in Istanbul" and displaying a pronounced fascination with Turkish culture and history. As the novel progresses, Azmi and Güzin start to realize that he is more than a mere distant relative of his namesake Vlad Dracula but is in fact the very same man. When we come to the section of the Dracula story where Doctor Resuhî (Van Helsing) explains his research on Dracula's history to the rest of the group, Seyfi extends this section to incorporate lengthy descriptions of historical battles between Vlad III and Mehmed II that are filled with patriotic, brave Turkish warriors battling against Vlad's cruel armies. Indeed, the notorious story of Turkish envoys having their turbans nailed directly to their heads by Vlad III after refusing to remove them is recounted as a symbol of national resistance designed to make the eventual defeat of Dracula even more emotionally resonant for the Turkish readership. Going well beyond a simple translation of *Dracula* into the Turkish language, Seyfi's novel remodels the text as a vehicle for expressing a distinctly nationalist take on the Dracula mythos. As Şehnaz Tahir Gürçağlar notes in her introduction to this book, *Kazıklı Voyvoda* was written soon after the Turkish War of Independence and Seyfi's adaptation can only be properly appreciated in light of that historical context. Muhtar's film, on the other hand, was produced nearly thirty years later in the early period of the Menderes government and removes many of the more overtly nationalistic elements of the adaptation and strips the story back to the core plotline—in the process often hewing closer to the Stoker novel than Seyfi's adaptation. Remarkably, unlike later adaptations such as Francis Ford Coppola's 1992 *Dracula* or Gary Shore's *Dracula Untold* (2014), the film contains no dramatizations of Vlad III's 15th century life and it wouldn't be until 1972 that Turkish cinema audiences would get to see Mehmed II face up to Vlad III in Natuk Baytan's largely fictionalized historical action film *Kara Murat: Fatih'in fedaisi* (Kara Murat: Fatih's Fedaration). It is therefore primarily in Seyfi's novel that we see this attempt to develop and strengthen the connection between the historical figure of Vlad III and Stoker's Dracula character as a way of localising the story for Turkish audiences.

While there are some question marks over whether the differences in Valdimar Ásmundsson's recently rediscovered Icelandic translation of *Dracula* are solely down to his imagination or are evidence of him working from an earlier Stoker draft, there are no such question marks over Seyfi's

Turkish adaptation. Going beyond the usual parameters of translation, Seyfi profoundly transformed the text for his own purposes and its patriotic content is clearly consistent with his subsequent historical novels. This book should therefore be recognized as a significant moment in the history of unauthorized transnational adaptations of Stoker's novel. Within film criticism, there is an increasing attention being paid to the numerous ways in which iconic characters such as Dracula have been adapted around the world within different national and cultural contexts. Beyond the canonical adaptations produced in America and Europe, Dracula has appeared on screen amongst Mexican haciendas in *El Vampiro* (*The Vampire*, 1957), as a symbol of the creeping threat of Westernization in Pakistan in *Zinda Laash* (*The Living Corpse*, 1967), fighting DC's Batman in the Filipino film *Batman Fights Dracula* (1967), and even battling against a resurrected Bruce Lee in the Hong Kong Brucesploitation film *The Dragon Lives Again* (1977). The character has proven to be exceptionally adaptable, appearing in numerous different forms and being utilized for a diverse range of ideological purposes. I hope that the recent translation into English of these Icelandic and Turkish literary adaptations of Dracula will similarly draw more attention to the various ways in which fiction authors around the world have reworked and remodeled Bram Stoker's tale. Given that Stoker's original novel was clearly rooted within the context of Victorian Britain and the prevalent anxieties at the turn of the century, it is important that we trace what subsequently happened when that character was displaced from that original context and adapted to other cultural and historical situations, for Dracula did not merely travel to Iceland and Istanbul but infected the entire world.

Poster for *Drakula İstanbul'da*

Atif Kaptan as Dracula
(Courtesy of Fatih Danacı)

Annie Ball as Güzin
(Courtesy of Fatih Danacı)

Güzin's Cabaret Number
(Courtesy of Fatih Danacı)

Annie Ball
(Courtesy of Fatih Danacı)

Osman Alyanak and Annie Ball
(Courtesy of Fatih Danacı)

Bülent Oran as Azmi and Kadri Ögelman as Dracula's Servant
(Courtesy of Ali Murat Güven)

ACKNOWLEDGMENTS

I would like to humbly and gratefully acknowledge the help of all the people involved in this project. Without their support, this book would not have become a reality.

My thanks to Neçip Ateş for his tireless translation efforts. Thanks to Şehnaz Tahir Gürçağlar, whose previous work on *Kazıklı Voyvoda* was a springboard for this endeavor, for contributing the introduction to this volume. Thanks to Iain Robert Smith, whose literature on transnational film remakes has been an inspiration to me, for composing the afterword. And thanks to Kim Newman, whose passion for all things Dracula knows no bounds, for his foreword.

Additionally, thanks to Can Yalçınkaya and Ali Murat Güven for their help in fine-tuning the translations of numerous Turkish words and idioms and contributing their considerable cultural and historical expertise, to Fatih Danacı for volunteering his personal archive of *Drakula İstanbul'da* publicity photos, to Meagan Rachelle for providing invaluable editorial assistance, and Alex Mitchell for his superb artwork.

This book has also benefitted from the advice and support of Ayşe Özcan, Kate Laity, and Carol Borden. Thank you all.

Çok teşekkür ederim!

—Ed Glaser

CONTRIBUTORS

Necip Ateş is a professional translator based in Turkey.

Ed Glaser is a Telly Award-winning filmmaker and film historian. He produces the online video series "Deja View" which showcases unauthorized foreign remakes of popular Hollywood films. He has written numerous essays on Turkish remake cinema and has been interviewed about the subject for CNN and the BBC.

Şehnaz Tahir Gürçağlar is a Professor in the Department of Translation and Interpreting Studies at Boğaziçi University, Istanbul. Her research interests are translation history and historiography, translation sociology, retranslation, periodical studies and reception studies. She is the author of *The Politics and Poetics of Translation in Turkey, 1923-1960*.

Kim Newman is an award-winning writer, critic, journalist, and broadcaster. His horror novels and short stories have won a number of industry "bests," including the Bram Stoker Award for his best-selling *Anno Dracula*.

Ali Rıza Seyfioğlu (1879-1958) was a Turkish translator, novelist, historian and poet. The author of some 29 books, his writing frequently featured nationalist themes. Formerly a naval officer, he composed several works on Turkish naval history. In addition to *Dracula*, Seyfioğlu also adapted Edgar Rice Burroughs's *The Beasts of Tarzan*, taking similar artistic license.

Iain Robert Smith is Lecturer in Film Studies at King's College London. He is author of *The Hollywood Meme: Transnational Adaptations in World Cinema*, and co-editor of *Transnational Film Remakes* and *Media Across Borders*.

Bram Stoker (1847-1912) was an Irish author, best known today for his 1897 Gothic novel *Dracula*. During his lifetime, he was better known as the personal assistant of actor Henry Irving and business manager of the Lyceum Theatre in London, which Irving owned.

www.ingramcontent.com/pod-product-compliance
Lightning Source LLC
Chambersburg PA
CBHW050448110726
47899CB00003B/859